# THE
# ALCHEMIST'S
# CHILDREN

## CAROLYN KILLION

**CALUMET
EDITIONS**

Minneapolis, MN, USA

CALUMET
EDITIONS

Minneapolis

FIRST EDITION OCTOBER 2016

For information, write to Calumet Editions, 8422 Rosewood Drive, Chanhassen, MN 55317

This is a work of fiction. Names, characters, places and incidents either are the product of the author's imagination or are used fictitiously. Any resemblance to actual persons living or dead, events, or locales are entirely coincidental.

Printed in the United States of America.

10 9 8 7 6 5 4 3 2 1

ISBN: 978-1-939548-56-6

Cover and interior design: Gary Lindberg

# THE ALCHEMIST'S CHILDREN

CAROLYN KILLION

# CHAPTER ONE

Wyatt slid his fingers along the smooth stone wall of his cousin's bedroom. His cousin had disappeared over fourteen years ago, and it was general knowledge that his bedroom was the off-limits part of the castle. Wyatt liked the feeling of risk that he felt when he snuck in to snoop around. He didn't do it often, for fear of being discovered.

"Catch this!" his brother Hunter hollered and tossed a flaming ball of bound rope at him.

Wyatt ducked as the ball spun past his head. He laughed as he lost his footing and fell hard against the dusty wall, causing a few stones to come loose and fall with him as he slid down. The fiery rope ball that had bounced against the wall above his head rolled toward the large dais bed on his left.

"Hunter. Get it before the coverlet catches fire," he yelled at his brother but Hunter had already run from the room. Wyatt sprang up and sprinted to the ball, kicking it back toward the wall before it could set fire to the bed covering. The ball bounced off the wall and rolled a few feet before coming to rest on the gray flagstone floor. It burned a few seconds longer and then began to smoke.

With a chuckle, Wyatt looked down at the smoldering ball, then back up and around the room. For nearly a decade and a half, all searches for his cousin, the heir to the throne, had been fruitless. Wyatt was sure he was dead. As next in line to the Dark Throne, his cousin Jeremias would not have left of his own accord. At least he would not have left without saying a word. Jeremias had been spending a lot of time the year before his disappearance patrolling the border lands. He had taken up residence there, to make the patrols easier, and would come back to visit the castle about once every two weeks. When he hadn't shown up for a visit after four weeks, his father, the Dark Leprechaun King, had sent a sentry patrol to check on him. They discovered he had been absent for almost a month. Search parties were sent out to all three Leprechaun Kingdoms, the Dark, the Light and the Ash, in an attempt to locate Jeremias. Now, nearing the fifteen year mark, still nothing.

The Dark King continued to send out search parties, but not as many or as often as the first few years. After five years with still no word or sign of his son, the Dark King had called his sister, Wyatt's mother, to the castle, and ordered her to bring her five sons. With Jeremias missing, Wyatt's oldest brother was being groomed as the new heir apparent. Even though it was hoped the prodigal son would return, the Dark King was making preparations in the event his son did not return.

Wyatt's oldest brother Jhett and second oldest Ian were now next in line for the Dark Throne. Wyatt was glad it was them and not him. He liked being ignored, able to go about his current business of mischief and merriment. Hunter was the youngest—a year younger than Wyatt—and also enjoyed the same youthful status. As spare heirs, they rated just above the lowest mongrel in residence at the castle. That served them just fine. As they weren't being groomed for positions of power, they were left to their own devices most of the time. The middle brother, Cayden, would sometimes join them. Although when he wasn't cavorting with Wyatt and Hunter in frivolous pursuits, Cayden spent a good deal of time with Jhett and Ian in more serious endeavors.

Jhett and Ian had become more solemn and distant since their move to the castle. The Dark King wanted strong heirs that thought and acted the way he did, and was determined through hard work to make them that way. He was succeeding. Wyatt's brothers had become harder over the past decade, almost as determined as the Dark King himself.

It wasn't that the Dark King was a bad king. He treated his people well and fairly. It was his contempt for anything that was not leprechaun. He believed the human world and humans should be servants to the leprechauns and that leprechauns should not waste their time guarding portals in and out of the human world, or keeping creatures not native to the human world out of it. The Dark Leprechaun Kingdom kept dragons from the human world, which was why their crest was that of a fiery red dragon. The clothing of the Dark Leprechauns was black, as dark as the hills of the dragon's world, and bright crimson red, much like the fire from the dragons they kept at bay.

The Dark Leprechaun Kingdom was craggy and mountainous, yet it wasn't dark like the dragon world. There were many snow-capped mountains, with small valleys in between, and as many sunny days as gloomy, cloudy ones. The Light Leprechaun Kingdom was in an area of lush, green rolling hills and meadows. Their crest was that of a Gargoyle, which they kept from the human world, and their clothing was green and brown. The Ash Leprechaun Kingdom was located amongst the islands of the great sea that surrounded both the Light and Dark Kingdoms. Their clothing was gray and brilliant blue, like the changing colors of the ocean, and their crest was a sea monster, which they kept in the seas and away from the human realm. The three kingdoms also kept other beasts and creatures from the human world, and other worlds they had treaties with, but these three beasts were the most troublesome and as such were the top priority of each kingdom.

Wyatt wasn't sure where the bitterness his uncle felt toward humans came from, but he didn't share it.

Although he'd never met a human, that didn't mean he thought he was better than one. They were just different. Even though humans were of similar height and build, the similarities ended there. Leprechauns had many more abilities that developed as they transitioned into adulthood.

Wyatt shook his head and returned his thoughts to the present room. By the door where the loose stones had fallen, something caught his attention. His gaze traveled up the wall until it settled on where the bricks had originated. He walked over to investigate further and found a hole about waist high. Tilting his head, he peered inside. An old scroll of some sort had been shoved through it. Wyatt tugged the scroll out, unfurled it and began reading the contents.

"Boy, what are you doing in here?" A loud snarl came from the entrance to his cousin's chamber. The Dark King! Wyatt stiffened and stood up straight. The Dark Leprechaun King stood taller than most, though not as tall as the tallest leprechaun. His height intimidated Wyatt. He tried to stay out of his uncle's notice as much as possible. That he was discovered in Jeremias's room could bode ill for him.

"I, um, I . . ." Wyatt stammered. He didn't know what to say. He knew he shouldn't be here. Instead of trying to explain further, he ran up to his uncle, threw his arms around his middle, and gave him a fast hug. He held the scroll tight in his fist.

"How dare you enter this room?" The Dark King began to bellow, but at the hug, his voice dropped into a normal, almost soft tone.

Wyatt stepped back and looked up at his uncle, who raised an eyebrow and stood silent a moment. The king took in slow, deep breaths. If Wyatt had just cowered and not said anything, his uncle might have hollered at him and tossed him from the room. Instead, with him risking a hug, his uncle had softened in a manner Wyatt rarely witnessed.

"Here, I found this." Wyatt handed the scroll to his uncle. They were the words of Jeremias, who had addressed the scroll to his father, explaining his reason for going to the human world. That his cousin had not returned to the Dark Kingdom meant that he was stranded there. Wyatt watched as his uncle read the scroll.

Once finished, the Dark King frowned, let the scroll coil back up, crushed it in one hand, then spun around and marched out the door. Wyatt stood there a moment, unsure of what to do. Halfway down the hall, his uncle paused and turned back toward him.

"Come, child. It's time to bring Jeremias home. I've an army to ready." The Dark King motioned for Wyatt to follow him. Wyatt didn't need a second invitation. He grinned, straightened his posture and ran toward his uncle.

# CHAPTER TWO

Her teacher was pontificating on the technological differences in warfare between World War I and World War II
when Gabriella first noticed a honey-blond ballerina in
a pink tutu go leaping past the classroom window. The
ballerina held a stick that had a long pink ribbon on one
end that she was waving around in circles with each leap.
Gabby glanced at the boy next to her, to see if he noticed
what was happening outside but he was looking at the
teacher and not out the window.

Gabby focused on the teacher and tried to ignore the
ballerina dancing outside. Most kids would have rushed
to the window to check out this new, strange phenome-
non. Not her. This type of stuff made her worry.

As the teacher continued to detail differences in the
machinery between the wars, a clown with bright orange
hair and a big red nose squirted the window with a fake
flower attached to the lapel of his brown patched jacket.
The clown wiggled his eyebrows and looked inside while
the ballerina continued to dance around behind him.

*Oh no, no, no, no, no, no,* Gabby thought to herself and hunched down further into her seat.

What sounded like an elephant trumpeted outside, heightening her growing fear. It appeared as if a circus had come to town and she was going to be its main spectator. Her palms became damp and she wiped them on the front of her jeans.

"That's odd." The teacher stopped her lesson and cocked her head to one side. "I thought I heard an elephant." As soon as the words had left her mouth, crashing symbols and the sounds of beating drums came from outside.

Mrs. Diddee walked over to the windows next to Gabby and peered out. "Wow!" she exclaimed and jumped back just in time. The clown shot the window with his water-filled flower again.

Gabby's classmates jumped up and ran over to see.

"Oh look," cried one. "It's a lion!"

"A hippopotamus!" shouted another.

"A marching band!" the twins in her class shouted in unison. They both played the clarinet in the high school band, so of course they would be interested in the marching band.

All her classmates were at the window, their faces pressed as close as they could get, oohing and aahing at the sights. Gabby was the only one still in her seat. She tried to slip further down, until she was almost ready to fall on the floor.

"Ok, class, everyone sit back down." Mrs. Diddee made a vain attempt to shoo everyone back toward their seats. She turned around the student closest to her, and gave her a gentle shove toward her chair.

"But Mrs. D," Alexander hollered over the ruckus of protesting students and blares of drums from the marching band, "it's a circus." Alexander was a short, brown-haired boy with braces.

"Yes Alexander, it does seem to be a circus, but please sit down." She pointed to his seat and he gave one last longing look outside before slinking back to his chair.

Most of the kids had resumed their seats when a knock came at the window. All heads swiveled in unison to see who was knocking. Gabriella's head was the only one that moved a different direction, down onto her desk.

Sure. This could be a coincidence; a circus could be outside for any reason. But she was sure the circus had come to her school for one reason only, and that was for her.

She peeked out from under the arm she'd stretched over her head as Mrs. Diddee walked to the window. It was a mistake. It confirmed her fear that this ruckus was in her honor. There, standing outside the window was a tall man with bright red hair. He had on a black suit with penguin tails, a snowy crisp white undershirt and a black bowtie. On his head was perched a large black top hat. He looked just like the circus ringmaster but she knew who he really was. He was a leprechaun.

While many believe leprechauns are tiny little creatures that dress in green and live in Ireland, she knew the truth. Leprechauns can look just like you or anyone else. They didn't live in Ireland, but rather a different realm.

"May I help you?" Mrs. Diddee had opened the window and was addressing the stranger standing outside.

"Yes, good woman, you may," the man said in a rich, Irish accent. "I am here to get Gabriella."

An instant flurry of breaths drawn in rushed around the room. All eyes were now on her.

"Gabriella?" her teacher asked him, directing a puzzled look her way.

"Yes, ma'am. I am in need of Gabriella," the tall leprechaun said as a monkey jumped onto his shoulder. Many of her classmates squealed in excitement at the appearance of this new creature.

The teacher turned, gave Gabby another puzzled look.

"Gabriella!" the leprechaun shouted when he saw her. Behind him the elephant trumpeted again and stepped into view. Riding on it was her eleven-year-old brother, Holden. He smiled and waved at her.

"Gabby, do you know this person?" Mrs. Diddee looked from her to the tall leprechaun and then back at her. The whole class was staring at her.

She stood up. "Umm . . . yeah," she muttered. "It's my uncle Robert."

Uncle Robert beamed at her as the monkey played with his collar.

"He was supposed to pick me up today." On the spot, she made up a little white lie. She'd not seen her uncle Robert in about six weeks and hadn't known he was going to be here today. Especially not with a full circus entourage in tow. Even if it wasn't real, it seemed real to the rest of the class and it was embarrassing to her in this moment of reality.

"Do you have a note?" her teacher frowned at her and crossed her arms.

"Ummm . . ." she said, and shifted her weight on her feet. She felt uncomfortable, very much on the spot. She didn't have a note because she hadn't expected to leave school early. That her uncle Robert was here in the middle of the day did not bode well. He only came on the weekends and it was rare that he ever interacted with them in public, especially when he was creating and utilizing deceptive imagery.

"I have one from her mother. She asked me to come and get Gabriella." With a pronounced flourish, her uncle handed a folded slip of paper through the window to Mrs. Diddee.

Mrs. Diddee glanced down and read the note. "Alright, Gabriella. You can go with your uncle." Her teacher folded the note back up and walked over to drop it on her desk. She folded her arms and gave Gabby's uncle a stern look. "Next time, for a dentist appointment, please go to the front office."

Sighing, Gabby closed her history book and put it inside her backpack. She slung it over her left shoulder and gave her uncle an equally stern stare.

"I'll meet you out front," she told him through clenched teeth, in the most grown up voice she could muster.

The entire class stared at her in amazement. Instead of meeting their eyes, she studied the multi colored speckles in the short classroom carpet as she walked to the door. If she looked up, she knew they would start asking too many questions for her to answer. She wanted to get out of there as fast as possible.

The bright sun blinded her for a few seconds when she stepped out in front of the school. While her eyes were adjusting, the entire menagerie of circus animals and performers circled her.

"What were you thinking?" She demanded of her uncle as she tossed her backpack on the ground. "Uncle Robert, I was at SCHOOL!"

He shrugged and gave her an ambiguous, lazy smile. "Your brother enjoyed the circus."

Raising her eyes, she looked up to where Holden was perched. His smile was as wide as a morning sunrise and just as brilliant. "Hey," she said to him. He smiled down at her and patted the top of the elephant's head.

Then she turned her attention back to her uncle. "You got him out of school too?"

"Yes," he said. He gave her a dazzling smile, but it didn't quite reach his eyes.

A clown pedaled past her on his unicycle, juggling orange balls as he went. The ballerina in pink spun in circles, following him. The rest of the circus milled around, each performing a unique act.

"Uncle Robert, please make the circus go away," she pleaded. "It's embarrassing."

Her uncle tipped his head at her and nodded once.

A fat lady approached her and began singing in a deep, throaty voice. Before her song could form any words, every performer and animal vanished.

"Very funny," Gabriella smirked. Her uncle stepped forward, intending to catch Holden, who had fallen from thin air once the elephant disappeared, but Holden landed in a crouch and then straightened. Unneeded, her uncle stepped back.

"Ugh," Gabby groaned, and picked up her backpack as she walked forward a few paces. It didn't matter that a whole circus had interrupted her class. In a few more moments, no one would even remember the event had happened. All her teacher would remember was that her uncle had picked her up for a dentist appointment. Not only did male Leprechauns have the ability to make you see things, they also had the ability to be forgettable.

"Gabriella." Her uncle placed his hand on her shoulder and turned her around to face him. "Aren't you wondering why I'm here?" He looked down at her, concern etched across his features. All traces of the humor from a few moments ago had gone.

"I was too upset over the circus to wonder," she answered. She'd not thought about it before, but why was he here? It must have to do with the reason her mom had not returned home.

She looked up at him and confessed, "Mom's been gone for six days now." Even though her mom had said it would only be for a day or two at the most, six days was longer than she'd ever been gone before. The night before she left, she'd come into Gabby's room and explained that she had something of great importance to do. Everything would be fine she'd told her, and trusted that Gabriella was old enough to take care of Holden and get both of them back and forth to school until she returned. Gabby had tried to question her, but her mom would not explain further. She said she was leaving because it was imperative that she take care of something. That was the last time Gabriella saw her.

"It is rumored the Dark King has captured her and is holding her prisoner." Her uncle looked at down at her, serious.

"So what're you doing here? How come you're not out saving her?" she asked, upset.

He crossed his arms over his chest and tilted his head down at her. "Now, Gabby, you know as well as I do that I cannot do that."

He was right. The Light Leprechauns could not enter the realm of the Dark Leprechauns. It was a very old truce, like the one the leprechauns had with the humans, to not invade or interfere with the kingdom of man.

"Do you know if she's okay?" she asked her uncle.

He shook his head. "Not for sure. All I know is where she's being held and that she's alive. My spies have that much information."

"Where is she? What was she doing?" Gabby asked. So many questions were piling up in her head and she spat them out as fast as they appeared. "What about us?" This worried her too. Who was going to take care of them while her mom was gone? What if she was never coming back? Even though she could take care of herself and helped her mom out around the house a lot, she was only fourteen. Would they have to go to foster care? Would they ever see their mom again?

Tears pooled in her eyes. Her uncle pulled her into his arms and gave her a big, tight hug. He pulled Holden against his side also. He smelled like the wet earth after the first spring rain and the ocean breeze on a warm summer day. It made her feel a little better but she was still worried.

"Don't fret too much, Gabriella," he said. "I have an idea." Uh oh. He had an idea. Now she was really worried.

"You have an idea?" she echoed as she pulled back and looked up at him. He gave her a big smile, full of bright white teeth.

"Yep," he said. "An idea."

"Oh great," she said. Holden slapped his forehead with his open palm for dramatic effect. They both knew how their uncle's ideas often turned out. He might be a grown prince in the land of leprechauns, but in the human world he was charming and mischievous. Too many times, his lack of knowledge of the human world had led to scrapes and mishaps.

"Nah. Don't worry." Telling her not to worry again was having the opposite effect. Gabby frowned at him in disbelief.

"Right," she muttered.

"I may not be able to enter the Dark Kingdom, but you and Holden can." His smile widened further.

Hope sprang alive within her. He was right. A full Light Leprechaun couldn't cross into the Dark Kingdom, but they could. Her shoulders perked up and she stood straighter. Wait. Could they? They'd never been to either of the Leprechaun Kingdoms before. They'd always lived with humans, in the Earth realm. Hope died a painful, gasping death inside her chest and her shoulders slumped back down.

"There is one small problem with your plan," she told him.

"What's that?" he asked.

"Our mom's a Light Leprechaun. We're her children. Even though we don't have magic, aren't we technically Light Leprechauns too? And we don't have magic, like you guys do." The children of leprechauns did not get their magic until after they became teenagers. It developed slowly and once you became an adult it would be at its full power. She worried that she and Holden would never get their power because they were half human. This would make them different in the leprechaun world. They would be at a disadvantage.

"Because you're a child and half human, I suspect that you're as mortal as can be," he told her.

"Yeah?" she asked, afraid to hope.

"Yes," he confirmed and continued to walk forward. "You will enter the pathway realm of the goblins to get to the Light Kingdom. I will have a select few trusted soldiers escort you to the borders of the Dark Kingdom. From there, I will meet you and we will get your mother."

Oh, wonderful. Her uncle's ideas were about as brilliant as driving a stock car without brakes on the highway in a Minnesota winter. She rolled her eyes.

"Once you enter the borders of the Dark Kingdom, I will have a reason to get both you and your mother," her uncle reiterated, ignoring her disrespectful mannerism as they walked.

"Are you nuts?" Gabriella asked. Entering the Dark Kingdom without escort or invitation, especially by one of the Light royal family, was tantamount to declaring war.

Her uncle gave her a hard look, and his red hair faded into a darker shade of chestnut brown, his original color. The king he was talking about wasn't any old king. This king was one of the High Kings of the leprechauns, like her grandfather and his father before him, the Light King.

"There are few other ways." Uncle Robert shrugged his shoulders and kept walking.

They had traveled a good distance away from her school and she noticed that Holden was starting to slow. Any minute now, her brother would start complaining. At least, she hoped he would so they wouldn't have to walk the entire way home. She glanced over at Holden, but he seemed content.

She stopped, huffed and crossed her arms over her chest. "Are we going to walk the entire way home?"

Her uncle walked a few more paces, ignoring her. Holden stopped and looked at her, hopeful. He knew the game she was playing.

After a few more paces, her uncle spun around on his heel and held his hands out to them. Gabriella and Holden both raced up to him and each took a hand. They loved when he did this. When they touched him, he was able to share and transfer a bit of his ability. In a blur of high speed, they ran home.

# CHAPTER THREE

"So your mom's been gone six days?" Uncle Robert asked as he grabbed the box of Lucky Charms cereal from on top of the fridge, and then opened the door to get the milk.

"Yeah," Holden said, "since last Friday night." He grabbed two bowls from the cupboard and set them on the table.

"You know that's weird, right?" Gabriella told her uncle, pointing out the cereal he was pouring into a bowl.

"That I like cereal?" He lifted an eyebrow at her and poured the milk.

"That you like that particular cereal. You know, being a leprechaun." Her uncle shrugged as he munched on a spoonful.

"Gabby," Holden said. He had a habit of saying her name any time he thought she was being silly. He tended to be serious quite often. Most of the time, he wasn't like other kids his age. Even though he could be really funny and endearing, he was serious more often than not. Holden turned his attention to their uncle. "Swordfight?"

Uncle Robert shrugged. "Only for a few minutes today. Once we're done, I want you to get your travel scabbard. Then I need you both to get your travel sacks and pack them with a change or two of clothes, enough for at least two days' time. The clothing I brought you. Leave a little room for the supplies I will gather for you in here." He gestured to the kitchen.

"Are we going to get our mom?" Holden asked. He let the spoon rest in his bowl and looked at his uncle.

"I hope so, Holden." Uncle Robert paused for a moment and looked at Holden, both their expressions serious.

"You hope?" Gabby pulled out a chair and sat down at the table with them. "What do you mean you hope?"

"I mean that I have every intention of finding your mother. I suspect I know where she is and it's not somewhere I'm able to go." Uncle Robert stood up, tossed his bowl back and drank the rest of the milk. He took the empty bowl and spoon over to the sink, rinsed them out and set them to the side. After a moment, he turned around.

"Gabriella, go change into the clothes I brought you before and pack a spare set like I asked. You too, Holden."

"Why can't you go? Where do you think my mom is?" Gabriella didn't move. If her mom was in a place her uncle couldn't go, then it probably wasn't a very good place. Her uncle was a prince; he could go almost anywhere.

"Gabriella, we will discuss this further, once you've changed. We need to make haste." He gave her a stern look and his tone allowed for no additional argument. He looked down at where Holden was still eating his cereal. "Holden, once you've changed, get me your side sword and your dagger."

Holden dropped his spoon into his cereal bowl, then pushed up and away from the table and loped off to his room. Gabriella looked at her uncle for another moment, and decided to ask one more question.

"Why can't we wear or take our own clothes?" she demanded.

"You will be out of place in them. Plus, the metal in your clothing isn't reinforced leprechaun steel," he told her. "Now, go change and get ready."

Scowling at him one more time, she turned and walked to her room.

She clenched her fists as she walked. Her palms were itchy and hot. They had been feeling that way off and on for a few weeks now. She wasn't sure if she was allergic to something or getting sick. A few times she had meant to tell her mom, but once the sensation went away, she forgot about it. The strange thing was, her scars felt that way too, hot and itchy at times, then the feeling would disappear.

Gabby opened the door to her room and went over to her dresser mirror. Lifting her hair away from the left side of her face, she turned to peer at herself. Angry scars zigzagged all over the left side of her head until they faded into her cheekbone. Her left ear was deformed. The top part and bottom lobe were gone and the scars were deepest on this side. She didn't remember much about the accident and fire; she just remembered her parents screaming and then searing pain. She vaguely remembered falling against the doorframe of the burning house while they had been escaping.

Her dad died in that fire. She had only a few memories of him smiling and laughing. Most of her memories involved him fighting and arguing with her mom. Her dad wanted to return to where he grew up, but her mom wanted to stay here in Minnesota. Holden hadn't been born yet. Her mom was pregnant with him when the house caught fire. The fighting had been the worst that night. The strange thing was, even though she remembered the searing, burning pain from falling into the doorframe, she didn't remember the actual fire. She remembered the doorframe being extremely bright, her dad holding her, her mom pulling her out of her dad's arms and then searing pain.

Despite wanting to ask her mom more questions and talk about it, she couldn't. Her mom would tear up and say she just couldn't talk about it, that she felt such an awful guilt that Gabby had gotten scarred in the fire and their dad had died. She cut Gabby off each time she brought up that night. One day, she promised Gabby, one day she would be able to talk about it more.

Gabby let her hair drop and opened a dresser drawer. She pulled out two pairs of thick, long creamy white socks and shut the drawer. With socks in hand, she walked over to the closet, where the dresses her uncle had brought for her over the years were hanging. Although simple in cut, they were gorgeous and reminded her of things people wore to Renaissance fairs. All were green, in varying shades, with gold threading and trim. They consisted of a chemise type dress of a lighter shade of green, then a darker overdress that partially covered the lighter one. She pulled two of the darker green dresses out, tossed them on the bed and reached to the closet floor for the dark brown leather lace-up boots that went with them. She pulled off her jeans, sat down on the floor, pulled on first the socks, then the boots.

Her mom used to sigh and shake her head when Uncle Robert brought clothes. They had so many already and her mom tried to explain that as they were never going back to Aurora—the leprechaun realm of three kingdoms she grew up in—the kids would not need these clothes. Uncle Robert would smile and say, "You never know," or, "They just might come in handy one day." It appeared that day was today.

She stood, pulled off her shirt and tossed it on her bed. Quickly, she pulled on the undergarment, then settled the second dress over it. Both skirts fell to her ankles, about an inch or two above the floor. Any longer and she'd get tripped up trying to walk.

Grabbing her green backpack off the hook by the door, she packed the other dress, an extra pair of socks, underwear, and a bra inside. As an afterthought, Gabby also tossed in her notebook, a few pens, a brush, hair bands, deodorant and chapstick. As she didn't know how long they'd be gone, she wanted to make sure she was prepared.

When a knock came at her door, Gabriella turned around. Uncle Robert opened the door and stepped into her room. "We cannot go directly to Aurora," he said.

"But I thought we were."

"I need to take you a different way. You are not full leprechauns so you are forbidden to enter the realm. Even though you are your mother's children and the king's grandchildren." He motioned for her to follow him as he turned and walked away.

"Then how will we get there?" Gabriella slung the backpack over her shoulder and followed him.

"There is a witch here, one who guards a portal to the goblin realm. The goblins are servants of the leprechauns and we can have you enter through this realm. While direct access from the human realm to the leprechaun realm is forbidden, you will be able to enter from the goblin realm. The goblins are extremely careful about who and what they let through their portals, as they are answerable to the leprechaun High Kings."

Her mom had explained this before. She vaguely remembered that there was a treaty between humans and leprechauns that was thousands of years old, before any written or recorded human history. The treaty dictated that leprechauns would not enter the realm of humans, unless to protect it, and humans would not enter the realm of leprechauns under any circumstances. It wasn't that the leprechauns feared humans, it was to protect the humans from leprechauns ever entering the human realm without cause and reason, as approved by the High Council of leprechaun kings.

Leprechauns were among the most dangerous creatures in existence in any of the worlds. The females, once they came of age, had the power of alchemy and the ability to open portals into different realms. They could turn any metal into gold, with the exception of leprechaun steel, which they formed and used. The male leprechauns possessed enhanced speed and strength and could make other beings see things that did not exist. It was a strange power of imagery that she didn't quite understand. It was what her uncle had done at school today when he created the circus.

# CHAPTER FOUR

Uncle Robert stopped in front of Gabriella and gestured to a house. She halted and waited for Holden to run back to them. After they had sped down to the south end of town, they had walked at a normal pace for the past four blocks. Holden was a few feet ahead, anticipating a longer journey. Before her uncle stopped, she thought they'd been headed for Starbucks, four blocks down. Uncle Robert loved Starbucks and that's where Gabriella assumed they'd been going, prior to accessing the portal. It usually didn't matter how dire a situation he was faced with, Uncle Robert always made time for a sugary, frothy, caramel-topped latte. That it was so close and he did not stop there first made her worry more.

Gabriella looked at the house before her. It was a bookstore of sorts, housed in a medium-sized Victorian house. There was nothing special to recommend it. The paint was white with no separate colored trim and the lawn was well manicured but simple and plain. The only designation it had marking it as a bookstore was the small wooden sign hanging from the front door by a thin cord. It read, "Aesop's Books." Aesop's Fables was a favorite book of hers and the name alone beckoned her to enter.

Holden ran past her and burst into the bookstore. Gabby jogged forward a few feet, ran up the steps and stopped. She had a backpack full of stuff and the storekeeper might not want it brought inside. Many bookstores did not like teenagers bringing in their book bags, because of possible theft. She let it slide off her shoulder and looked around for a place to put it.

"Oh, that won't be necessary," a soft feminine voice drifted out to her.

"No?" Gabby questioned and turned around, a bit confused.

"You can bring it inside." A pretty woman with fuzzy, bright red hair stepped into view, just inside the entrance. She had on a calf-length summer dress of bright yellow, one that should have clashed with her hair, but instead blended with the long, flowing locks.

"Yeah?" It was not often that a shopkeeper was so liberal with teenagers.

"Yes, please, come in. Both of you." She gave them a big smile that showed perfect teeth and took a few steps backward.

"Great." Gabby smiled back, lifted her bag back up and walked in past the woman.

Large, full built-in bookcases met her eager stare. From floor to ceiling, they encompassed the entire perimeter of the room. She walked into the next room and it was similar to the first, except that huge, overstuffed pillows littered the floor along with an old fashioned wooden train set, set up in a figure-eight style. Holden was zipping the three-car train around and around the track.

"Are you looking for something in particular?" The shopkeeper asked from behind her. Gabriella turned and saw that she was favoring both her and her uncle with a bright smile.

"I'm not sure," Gabby answered as she looked up at her uncle.

With a sudden gasp, the woman's brilliant smile dimmed and she tilted her head down. "Your highness, I did not recognize you. " She bent at the waist, lifted the ends of her skirt and executed a small curtsy.

Uncle Robert waited for the woman to finish her curtsy and look up at him. He lifted his hand, palm toward her and waved off any further words she might have spoken. "We need passage through the portal to the goblins' realm," he said.

Gabriella was stunned. Before this moment, she had always thought of her uncle as just her uncle. When he came to visit, he would be dressed in his standard clothing of the leprechaun court, the dark green tunic with gold trim, the buff-colored breeches and dark brown leather boots. Gabriella never paid much attention, unless they went out in public, to a park, restaurant, Starbucks or anywhere else. He'd usually get odd stares or the random "going to a costume party or the Renaissance fair" comment, but no one ever paid him much more notice than a few cursory glances. This witch recognized him and that had never happened before.

"Yes, your highness." The woman bobbed her head at him. Gabriella lifted an eyebrow at her uncle. He no longer looked like her fun-loving relation, but a cold, serious man. This was a man she did not know.

Perplexed and suddenly wanting a bit of distance from the situation and the odd feeling in the bottom of her stomach, Gabriella turned and wandered to the book shelves closest to her. The books were all large and bound in assorted earth tone covers. Stepping closer, she peered at the spine of one. It bore fine silver lettering on a dark gray background, "Fairies at Midnight." She frowned and read the title of the one next to it, "Fairy Mythology." Gabby stepped back and glanced at the section. It all seemed to deal with fairies, in some manner or another. Fairies and Water Nymphs, Fairy Dieting, Fairy Buttons, Fairy Crocheting, Fairy Dating. Wait? Did that just say Fairy Dating? She wrinkled her nose and turned around, taking in another section. Gnomes. Goblins. Gremlins. She walked to the next section. Warlocks, Werewolves, Witches, Wizards and wait, there it was, a whole section on Wizard dating. How to Date a Werewolf on a Full Moon Using Only Simple Spells, Dating after Moonlight Spell Casting, Dating Disasters of Minor Wizards, and more. Gabby almost laughed aloud. The titles were preposterous and hilarious at the same time.

What type of bookstore had they stepped into? As Gabriella turned to ask, a sudden blast of light blinded her. The floor trembled and she had to grab the edge of a shelf to keep from falling. Both the witch and her uncle gasped.

Gabby stood there a moment until the light receded and her vision cleared. Her palms and the side of her face burned hot. Holden had come to stand next to her. The beautiful shopkeeper and her uncle now stood before her too. The shopkeeper was frowning.

"The children need passage now," Uncle Robert said and lifted his hands. He removed a large gold ring from his right hand. "Do you have string, twine, anything to tie this with?" he asked the shopkeeper.

The shopkeeper hurried into a different room. Uncle Robert lifted the ring to show them.

"This is my signet ring. It is the ring the heirs to the Light Throne carry. Your mother and my father both have one. I'm giving this to you. If you encounter any trouble, show the goblins and ask for safe passage to the Leprechaun Light Kingdom. My men will be waiting for you next to the portal.

"But what if they aren't there?" Gabriella interrupted.

Robert frowned and continued: "If for any reason they are not there, follow the path to the castle. Do not step off the path or follow any smaller forks away from it.

Stay on the large main path and it will go directly to the castle. Again, ask for entrance and show them this ring if you are questioned."

The witch returned with a ball of twine. She pulled off a length of a little over a foot and handed it to Uncle Robert. He slipped the ring through, tied the ends into a knot, and tested it for strength and durability. Once he was sure the knot would hold, he slipped the newly formed twine and ring necklace over Holden's head, tucking it under Holden's tunic.

"Go swiftly through this portal and head straight to the goblin Bentley's manor. The witch will give you further instructions on how to find it. I must go. Now." With that, he hugged them each tightly and then rushed out the door.

"I don't think you should let the children go through alone," the witch called after him, but it was too late. He'd already gone. The witch looked back at Holden and Gabriella, worry marring her brow.

"You need to hurry." She took Gabriella's hand and began pulling her toward the door. "Come."

"Why? What's going on?" Gabby didn't understand what was happening. She knew they had to go through the portal, but she didn't understand what had just happened. She also didn't know how they would get to the goblins' realm or what they would say when they did.

"A large portal was just opened into the human realm. From your uncle's reaction, an unauthorized portal, it seems," the witch said.

"One like we are going through?" Holden asked.

"No, the one that just opened was extremely large. One person could not open a portal that large. It would take quite a few leprechauns to create one that size. No portal like that has been opened in my lifetime." The witch shook her head. Deep lines creased her brow. "Portals like that are used for only one thing."

"What?" Gabriella and Holden asked simultaneously.

"Invasion. Something large coming through. When one that big is opened, the ripple effect can be felt through all the realms," the witch said. Then she reached forward and pulled hard at Gabby's hand, causing her to lurch forward. Gabby pulled back with equal force and righted herself.

"Child." The witch motioned Holden forward, toward her.

"Listen carefully, both of you. Once inside the portal, go to the red house, about four blocks down, on the right. This is the house of Gildseth and Bentley, the goblins. They have access to the gate that will take you to the realm of the leprechauns. Although you may enter, don't stay long. It is never a good idea to linger in the realm of goblins. Oh, and they will want payment but not the monetary type."

"What?" Gabriella seemed to have a recurring theme of monosyllabic questions and responses.

"Hurry! Please. You must get there before dark and you don't have much time." With that last statement, she turned and hurried to the bookshelf on the far side of the room. Gabriella frowned at Holden, perplexed. The shop-keeper pulled down a small dark brown box from the top of the shelf and reached inside. She pulled something out and then put the box back on the shelf.

"Here," she said as she hurried back and they all looked at what she held in her palm. "Offer this as payment." The witch handed Gabby a few small smooth, shiny oblong objects. They looked like small metal stones. "This should serve well enough as payment for the goblins."

The witch turned luminous eyes toward them. "I can't help you anymore. Follow me now." She walked them over to a door on the opposite side of the wall and freed a necklace from inside her clothing. On the thin, metal chain was an old, burnished skeleton key. Not re-moving the key or chain from her neck, she bent down, put the key into the door, and paused. "You are young leprechauns; keep your wits about you." She twisted the key, stood back upright and opened the door. There was nothing special beyond the door. It looked like the en-trance to the bookstore, with the same white wooden deck and sidewalk leading up to the store. At the witch's urg-ing, Holden and Gabriella stepped through. Then the door slammed shut behind them.

# CHAPTER FIVE

Gabriella and Holden walked down the steps away from the bookstore.

"What in the heck was that all about?" Gabriella asked. "Did you hear her call us leprechauns?"

Holden wasn't paying attention to her. He was looking around. She followed his gaze. They were no longer on Grand Ave, where they had entered the bookstore. They were, but were not. The buildings were similar, but different, in a vague sort of way. They were all closed and no one else was outside. The look of everything seemed off. It took her a few seconds to realize what was different.

It was reminiscent of the moment between day and night, when the sun touches the horizon and casts the whole land into a blazing wash of firelight. Things become surreal in an ultra-rich fabric of colors. Yellows become gold, reds deepen into brick and blues bleed into varying blends of black.

She stepped forward, away from the bookshop and out on the sidewalk. It was no longer a smooth cement pattern but a patchwork of stones.

After she took a few more steps out onto the cobblestoned sidewalk, she felt a feeling of tranquility settle deep inside her. It was a wonderful, comforting feeling and she resisted the urge to smile and sigh. The desire to find the nearest patch of grass, to curl up and sleep, was almost irresistible. She looked down at Holden and realized that he had the same contented smile. This was strange. She wanted to relax, to enjoy and take in the surroundings, but the shopkeeper's warnings were fresh in her mind.

"Holden, we should go to the house like she told us to." Gabby turned to get his opinion.

"I guess," he seemed calm and relaxed. Not worried at all.

"Yes," she said. "We should, before we decide we don't want to."

"I already don't want to." He tilted his head on his shoulders, first one way then the other, stretching his neck out.

"I think we should go. Come on." She started down the path, heading to the right, in the direction the woman had given her. Although hesitant, Holden followed.

They had gone past a few houses when they saw two men step out onto the path ahead of them. They were deep in conversation and walking at a brisk pace. Maybe they would know where the goblins' house was located.

"Excuse me, sirs," Gabby said loudly, hoping to get their attention. They either did not hear or ignored her and kept up their fast pace. They were both dressed in a deep, wine-colored purple. From their suit jackets to their slacks to even their shining purple shoes, it was all a very dark shade of midnight purple. A color you would expect a king to be robed in. It should have stood out in dark contrast to the world around them, but instead it blended very well and seemed almost normal. They both had on matching purple top hats and carried briefcases, although these were black.

They turned and went toward a gorgeous little cottage, painted barn-red with green shrubs lining the walk. Flowers of all colors peeked out of window boxes .

A red house, to the right and a few blocks down, Gabriella thought. It struck her suddenly. This must the goblins' house. The first of the men to reach the house set his briefcase down and put his hand into his pants pocket. He brought out a set of keys and turned one in the door.

She broke into a light jog. "Sirs," she called again. This time, the one waiting turned to look at them.

"Hi," she said, coming to a stop before him, a little breathless.

"Hello," he responded, slow and deliberate. His gaze took them in, his gaze sharpening for a moment. Then his features relaxed. "May I help you?" he asked. The man behind him paused for a moment before he went inside, leaving the door open in his wake.

The man before her was neither tall nor short. She was five foot seven inches and he was an inch or maybe two taller than she was. He had deep brown eyes and dark hair that matched. His face was a bit round but his nose was long and thin. His frame was thick but he was not fat.

"Please. We are looking for Gildseth and Bentley." She extended her hand in greeting.

"I am Gildseth." He ignored her hand and she let it drop.

"Great," she said, her smile fading. He was looking at her, waiting. She didn't know what else to say.

"Umm, I'm looking for a gate," she stumbled, not quite sure what to ask.

"A gate," he repeated.

"Yes," she said and looked at him a little closer. The feelings of warmth and happiness that she'd had began to dissipate.

He raised an eyebrow.

"A gate home. What I mean is a portal to the leprechaun realm." This felt like a game of sorts, although she was not sure there was a set of rules. There might be, but she was unaware of them.

"Ahh, now we are getting somewhere." He stood up to his full height and looked down at her.

"Can you help us?" she asked.

"I might be able to," he said. He still clutched his briefcase. The daylight was fading around them and little lamplights along the path were starting to illuminate.

"Thank you. We'd really appreciate it." She nodded at him. He held her gaze a moment, then glanced at Holden, spotting the string tied around his neck.

"The necklace, may I see it?" he asked.

Gabby looked at Holden, expecting him to argue. He just stood there, not saying anything. His simple compliancy bothered her.

Putting her hand on Holden's shoulder, Gabby stepped forward and addressed Gildseth: "I'm sorry, the necklace is private and personal."

Even though her uncle had instructed her to show the signet ring for safe passage, the situation was making her nervous. She didn't want to show the ring yet.

Gildseth shifted his attention from her to Holden, then back to her again. His smile was quite sincere in a somehow very insincere manner. His head swiveled around slowly to assess Gabby. He tilted it down a little to the right and his dark violet eyes gazed into hers.

"And if I do not allow you to enter without seeing what is on the string?" His speech was slow and deliberate. It was as if the question was more important than determining admittance for a mere view of a necklace. In a flash, Gabby saw his features elongate a bit, become a touch more severe. His nose, chin and forehead all seemed to sharpen and protrude to a point. This terrified her and made her stomach muscles clench. She wanted to grab Holden, leap back and put distance between them and this creature.

Instead, she shoved down her fear and offered him a brilliant smile. She felt like an idiot, but she smiled nevertheless. Although she was asking him for help, she needed to convince him that their need was not as great as it really was.

Gabby tilted her head to match his and said something that she thought might sound stupid, but she didn't know what else to say: "Then you would miss the opportunity of our company."

In that instant she knew that this creature wanted her blood. That nothing would make him happier than to be able to grab her throat with both hands, twist with an inhuman strength and sever her head from her shoulders, just so he could feast upon the hot spray gushing forth. Even so, she felt calm and almost giddy. Here they were, stranded in a strange land that was not quite their own and she was near laughter. There was something odd about this realm and it was affecting both her and Holden.

The shroud of comfort and peace was a hard one to shrug off, but she had to find the chaos in the moment and hold on to it. Not only for her survival but that of her brother. Holden and she were both affected and Holden was rarely this well behaved. By now he should have been zipping from one shiny object to the next, touching and examining and making a general nuisance of himself in the most inappropriate manner. As hard as their mom tried to instill manners, he reigned superior in retaining pandemonium for his own particular personality.

That he was being quiet, calm and well-mannered alarmed her further. To test the point she reached down for his hand and held it. He grasped it without question, proving her point. He was be-spelled in some manner. It led her to wonder why she wasn't affected as badly. Even though she was fighting feelings of abnormal joy and contentment, she was pretty much herself. Before she could ponder further, Gildseth dipped into a noble half bow and with a flourished rotation of his arm, bid them enter.

Gripping Holden's hand tighter in her now-sweating one, Gabby stepped across the threshold. She half expected to be struck by lightning or a heavy candelabrum of sorts or to have something macabre happen. But nothing did. They merely strolled into the house and stopped in the small foyer, awaiting further instruction and invitation into the home.

Gildseth took off his top hat and hung it on a peg where a matching purple one resided. The other one must belong to Bentley, the gentleman who had entered before them. Below the top hats, at about the middle of the wall was another set of pegs. A purple jacket hung from one. Gildseth leaned his briefcase next to the wall and shrugged out of his matching jacket, then hung it below his top hat.

"Bent," Gildseth called out, "we have guests." He paused to pick up his briefcase and stepped through the doorway to another room.

Bentley poked his head around the doorway Gildseth stepped through. His glossy brown hair poked out at odd angles, like he had shoved his fingers in the mess and twisted his strands every which way.

"Welcome," he said.

Holden only looked at him and smiled. Unsure what to do, Gabby said, "Thank you," back to him.

"Staying for dinner?" he asked as he stepped into the foyer. He had on a white apron with bright red cherries on it. The sleeves of his purple button-down shirt were rolled up past his elbow.

Dinner sounded wonderful and they were famished. The offer of food seemed to snap Holden out of his lull.

"Oh yes. I'm starving!" he exclaimed and dropped Gabby's hand.

"Um, well. I'd love to, but . . ." Gabby's voice trailed off. She wanted to stay and eat but somehow it just didn't seem right. Persephone jumped to the forefront of her thoughts. She had broken the proverbial bread with Hades and become trapped. Gabby didn't want something like that or worse to happen to them.

"But?" Bentley quirked his eyebrows at her.

"My mom has a wild rice soup waiting for us at home." She frowned as she lied to him, almost repentant.

"Oh, that sounds delicious." He winked and smiled and clearly didn't believe her for a second. "Come sit with us for a while then."

"Of course." She smiled back and made sure hers was more sincere. If this was a game of cat and mouse, then she wanted to be the mouse that escaped.

41

He led them into the next room, which opened up into a bright, sunny kitchen. Gabby gasped in awe and stood still. In front of them was a wonderful, cozy space that she did not expect. She'd thought that their kitchen would be dark and dank with a fireplace at one end and a plank table down the center. Something more medieval and rustic. Instead, this one had big white cabinets lining the walls on three sides and matching countertops filled with assorted appliances. Lemon yellow curtains adorned a picture window in front of a large stainless steel sink and a modern dishwasher whirred in action next to it. A large, round wooden table stood in the center. It had frilly lemon-colored doilies scattered all over it, with a tea service in the middle and dinner plates set at each chair.

Bentley gestured toward the table. "Sit down, make yourselves comfortable." He pulled out a chair for Holden and then turned to attend a skillet on the gleaming white stove.

Gabby sat in the chair closest to Holden. He just smiled and looked around the kitchen.

"Can I get you anything to drink?" Gildseth asked as he entered the kitchen.

"Sure," Holden said.

"Ah, thanks, but we can't stay too long." Gabby shook her head no at Holden. He shrugged. Even though he was not as passive as before, there was still something amiss.

Gildseth brought a pitcher of water to the table and sat down next to them.

You don't want to partake in anything we have to offer?" he asked.

Gabby thought for a moment. Was this a question or a test? She looked at Holden, hoping for some help from him. He just sat there, slightly grinning.

"It is not that we don't want to accept what you have to offer," she said, "but we don't want to take more than you are already giving us." She hoped this was the correct thing to say.

"What we are already giving you?" Gildseth's gaze never wavered from hers. She desperately wanted to break away, look at something else, but she was held, trapped by his stare.

"A way through the portal," she answered.

He smiled and looked away.

"Sausages?" Bentley said, placing a bowl of steaming gray breakfast sausages in the center of the table. He reached over to the drawer nearest Gabby, withdrew a small set of silver tongs and put them in the sausage dish.

Gildseth took the tongs and placed a few sausages on his plate. Bentley sat down next to Gildseth and did the same. They both took a moment to breathe in the scent of the meat before they began eating.

"How did you come to be here?" Gildseth directed his question at her.

"We were in Aesop's Bookstore when another portal, a very large one, was opened." She wanted to act like she knew exactly what she was talking about, when in actuality, she had no clue.

"Ah, Tisha's store, a lovely little place," Bentley said as he chewed.

"Yes, we liked it," Gabby agreed.

"I liked the train," Holden piped up.

Both men smiled at Holden and continued to eat.

"What do you do?" Gabby asked. She wondered what type of work would require a goblin to carry a briefcase and the question just popped out.

Gildseth and Bentley stopped eating and looked at each other. "We're advisers to the king," Gildseth answered in his slow manner. They resumed eating.

King? My grandfather, the king of the leprechauns or another king? It was odd. Gabby wanted to shout that there was no king but she didn't. Instead she played along and said, "Oh. Do you enjoy it?"

"We do," Bentley said.

"What do you do?" Gildseth asked her.

"I'm a student, I go to school," she said.

"A fine profession, being a student," Bentley said. Gildseth agreed.

"I am too," Holden interjected.

This made both men smile. It was simple banter and Gabriella was becoming relaxed again. She glanced through the picture window to the gorgeous setting outside. There was a large yard out back with lush trees scattered throughout. The sun was shining and a hammock was strung between two trees closest to the kitchen window.

Wait a moment. She pushed back her chair, stood and walked over to the window. The sun was high in the sky. Just a few moments ago, at the bookstore, it had been nearing sunset. They had to get out of here now. This was a setting for something sinister and they were in an unknown realm. They were not where they were supposed to be and that terrified her.

Struck with sudden inspiration, she looked around and pulled open the drawer nearest to her. It held an assortment of utensils. At the front, underneath a few wooden spatulas were a dozen razor blades. She remembered what the storekeeper said. These men were expecting payment of some sort and somehow, the metal rocks did not seem sufficient. Plus, she didn't have much money and was sure that it was useless here, wherever here was. She knew what these men wanted. They wanted blood. She'd give them some.

Careful not to cut herself, Gabriella lifted a razor blade and held it up for Gildseth to see.

"May I use this?" she asked, keeping any expression from her face. This was hard. She was an emotional person and as such didn't have an actor's face. Usually, every feeling raced across her features in its haste to snitch her out.

"Of course," he said with a single nod.

"Might I offer our thanks and give payment for your assistance?" she asked, nervous because she was making it up as she went. Both men gave her a puzzled look but kept smiling their vicious little smiles.

"You may," Gildseth said. Bentley nodded in agreement and popped another sausage into his mouth.

Gabriella stood and lifted Holden's left hand. Quickly, she made a small slice on his forefinger. Blood oozed out in a perfect oval. Leaning over, she took from beside the teapot one of the many small saucers. She then held Holden's finger over it and squeezed out a few drops. They hit the saucer with small splashes. He didn't protest or ask her why she was cutting him and creating a mess of blood on the saucer. The thick ruby liquid pooled in the center of the saucer and coated the edges of the cup indentation in the middle. Looking at the blood made her feel queasy, but it was not the sight of it that did so. It was the action of cutting through the flesh of a loved one and squeezing from it that which sustained life, even if it was only a very small amount. Shaking her head, she set his hand down and proceeded to make a small incision into her thumb. She squeezed drops of her blood into the saucer also, matching the amount she had taken from Holden. Once she thought there was enough, she jammed her thumb into her mouth, to try to stop the stinging, and pushed the saucer toward the goblins.

Gildseth and Bentley looked at the plate. Bentley was slow to smile as he dipped his finger in the blood and then brought it to his lips. He opened his mouth and slid his finger inside, closing his eyes.

Suddenly, his eyes sprang open and widened. "Gildseth," he said as he looked at Gabby.

Gildseth dipped his finger in, then sucked on it also. He never closed his eyes but they widened too.

He let his finger drop and both he and Bentley sprang to their feet. Both goblins seemed nervous and unsure. In a breath of a moment, all the fear that she'd felt before disappeared. It shifted from them being afraid of goblins to the goblins being afraid of them. It didn't make sense. Yet it didn't need to at that moment. It mattered more that they got out of there and fast.

"Your highness," he gave her a short bow. Bentley bowed toward Holden. Holden stood and walked over to stand next to Gabby.

"We need to get through the portal to see our uncle." Gabby said, still struggling with the sudden shift in power. She wanted to leave immediately, before the fear shifted again and the danger returned.

"And you are not opening your own portal?" Bentley asked, his words slow and measured. Gabriella sensed that she was being tested.

"No, it is not authorized. I'd prefer to follow proper channels," she said and gave the goblin a clipped nod. If he was going to call her a highness, then she was going to act like it. If it got them through this situation, then she was determined to win an Oscar.

"Yes, your highness," Bentley's features seemed less taut, her answer apparently appeasing him.

"Really, we must go see our uncle now. It is extremely important." Gabriella stepped closer to Holden, who'd been silent through the exchange.

He chose that moment to lift the ring from where it had been hanging inside the tunic.

"Our uncle is expecting us," he said and lifted the ring for the goblins to see.

"We apologize for any delay that was caused. Again, thank you for the offering. We had thought you to be human. We did not realize." Gildseth gave Gabby yet another small nod. Bentley did the same. They seemed to be apologizing for something more than just the delay. Gabby nodded back at them and Holden did the same.

"Let's get you home." Bentley took off his apron and tossed it on the counter, next to a gleaming white toaster. Gildseth gestured to the hallway that led off the kitchen.

Holden and Gabby followed Gildseth and Bentley down the hallway and through a door that looked like it led to a garage. It didn't. Instead of opening up and revealing a vehicle, assorted bikes and other miscellaneous items, it opened up to lush, rolling green hills. A dirt path led from the doorway and meandered up and through the hills.

It must be the path that Uncle Robert had told them about. She peeked her head on either side of the door. There was no one there to meet them. She turned back around to where Bentley and Gildseth stood behind her.

"Thank you very much," she said to Gildseth and Bentley.

"You're welcome," Bentley answered, slightly bowing toward her again.

"Yes, you are," Gildseth agreed. He mimicked Bentley's slight bow. Both goblins stood on the threshold, not crossing it. Holden and Gabriella stepped through and the door closed, leaving a large, rounded boulder behind them, not a door.

# CHAPTER SIX

Gabriella stood on the dirt road, which led out from the boulder, went straight for about a quarter mile, and then started to bend and snake back and forth until it wound out of sight through the gentle rolling hills. She saw no trees. Except for the green grass that waved softly in the light breeze, the hills were bare.

She looked at Holden.

"Should we wait?"

"Uncle Robert said someone would meet us here," Holden said as he kicked at the dirt.

"Yeah," she agreed and turned back to the dirt road. It was narrower than the roads back home, only wide enough to fit four people walking, shoulder to shoulder.

"But no one is here." Holden waved his arms.

"Maybe we should wait a bit." Gabby stepped off the path and walked over to a grassy spot next to the boulder. She lowered herself to the ground and sat crossed legged. Holden followed and flopped down next to her.

"You'd think that if this was a portal or gate to this world, someone would be here guarding it at least," Holden said. He ripped out a blade of grass and rolled it between his fingers. "If I were the king, or Uncle Robert, I would have all portals guarded."

"Maybe," Gabby said. She continued to look down the road, hoping someone would show up to meet them.

"Seriously, think about it. Look how easy it was for us to come through. What if someone bad wanted to come through? No one is here to defend the kingdom."

"Well, I don't know that it was that easy. We were shown where the portals were and someone led us through each time," Gabby said.

"True, but someone else could do that also. It is possible," Holden said.

"I guess," Gabby said, not really paying attention to him.

Holden was frustrated his sister didn't agree with him. He thought it was too easy to walk through portals from one realm to another. Even though it was his first time, the way they got here proved that anyone else could do it just as easily. He got to his feet.

"I think we should start walking down the road towards the castle. Something must have happened," he said.

"I don't know. Maybe we should wait a while longer." Gabby looked at him. She didn't get up.

"What if that big portal opening is the reason no one is here?" Holden asked. "I think we should start walking instead of waiting for someone. They might not come for a long time, or even at all." He offered a hand to Gabby. She placed her hand in his and he helped pull her to her feet. Once standing, she reached back down to grab her backpack.

"Alright, let's go." She slipped her arm through one handle of her backpack, slung it on her back and then slipped through her other arm. She didn't know how long they had to walk.

"Holden, set the metal stones down," she told him.

"Why?" he asked, confused. They were supposed to be payment for the goblins. His sister had paid them in blood instead.

"Because we were supposed to give them to Bentley and Gildseth. We didn't. I think we should set them down here, in case they come this way. They will see them and then, in a way, we did give them their fee," she told him.

He nodded and reached into his pocket to retrieve them. He rubbed them a few times before he knelt down and set them on the ground. Holden straightened back up and they started along the path in silence.

After not too long, they crested the hills.

"Wow," Holden said as he stood at the top of a hill.

"I know, right," Gabriella said in response. She couldn't believe what she was seeing. It looked like a scene out of a fantasy movie. The dirt road stretched through a few more rolling hills before it straightened out and led up to a large, walled castle. It appeared to be like the Norman castles she'd studied in history class, but that was where the resemblance ended, due to the sheer size. It was about ten times wider and larger than any pictures of castles she'd ever seen before. There was an even larger outer wall that surrounded many smaller buildings, a wide bailey and in the center of it all stood the imposing, large slate gray castle. It had square towers on all four sides and was constructed from what appeared to be stone. From their vantage point, she could see little dots that looked like soldiers standing sentry on top of the castle walls, behind the parapet.

In the front of the large stone outer wall surrounding the castle, there was a double wooden gate. Two garrisoned men stood in front, guarding them. There were also more dirt paths that led directly to the castle gates.

"Do you think this is where mom grew up?" Holden asked.

"I don't know. I think so." Gabby continued to stare down at the castle scene before her.

"Why does she live in the human world if she could live here?" Holden mused. He didn't understand. If he grew up here, he'd want to stay. It was incredible. He hadn't even been inside the castle yet, but thought it was amazing.

"Maybe it's because of us, because we're part human?" Gabriella shrugged. Their mom must have had a good reason. Holden looked at her but didn't say anything. After a moment, he stepped forward and began to make his way down the path toward the castle. Gabriella sighed and followed him.

As they approached the castle gates, Gabby and Holden noticed that there was a flurry of activity happening inside and out. The closer they got to the castle, the more activity they saw. There were two paths that led to the castle from opposite directions. One was the path they were on, and from the other, in the opposite direction, riders on horses were approaching and going through the gates. The guards did not stop to talk to these riders, but quickly opened the gates, let them through and then closed the gates again. When the gates were open, they could see many horses and soldiers going in many different directions.

"I wonder if the castle is usually this busy," Gabriella wondered. She couldn't imagine the castle being chaotic all the time like this. If it were, that might explain why their mom didn't live here.

As they approached the gates, another thunder of hooves approached from the left path and four green and brown clad men on horses approached the gates. The guards threw the gates open to allow them passage. Gabriella and Holden paused a few steps back to keep from being trampled.

Once the guards closed the gates, they stepped forward. The guards looked them over, but didn't say anything. They were both tall, as tall as Uncle Robert, and their faces betrayed no emotion. They didn't appear to be surprised to see two kids standing in front of them.

"We're here to see Prince Robert," Holden said.

"No admittance is allowed to the castle at this time for audience with the royal family." The guard on the left looked down at them.

"Our uncle is expecting us," Gabriella told the guard.

"Your uncle?" Both guards spoke in unison. They quickly exchanged a glace and then looked back at the children. This time their faces showed surprise.

"Yes, Prince Robert is our uncle," Holden said. He stood as tall as possible, daring the guards to disagree with him. He had the signet ring hidden in his shirt, but didn't want to show it yet. He wanted to make these men understand who he was just by his presence.

Before the guards or the children could speak further, a shout came from the ramparts to the right of the gates. "Gabriella, Holden, hello!" A girl between their ages with long, dark brown hair was waving down to them.

"You made it!" she shouted down. "Colm, let them through. My dad's expecting them." She looked down at the guard who had spoken to them. Then she disappeared.

"Yes, milady," the guard the girl had called Colm said, but he was speaking to himself at this point. He and the other guard each grabbed a door handle and pulled the large gates open, to allow Gabriella and Holden to pass. The girl was waiting just inside, hopping up and down. She had on a green dress with gold trim nearly identical to what Gabriella wore.

"Oh wow, oh wow, oh wow. I've been waiting for this day for what seems like forever!" she said, continuing to hop up and down as they walked through the gates.

# CHAPTER SEVEN

Once Gabriella and Holden stepped inside and the gates closed behind them, the girl ran forward and threw her arms around Gabby. She gave her a quick hug, let her go, then turned and hugged Holden just as quickly. Afterwards, she stepped back and smiled.

"Who are you and why did you hug me?" Holden asked. He stood stiffly. A confused look furrowed his brows. His uncle's men had not met them, and now here stood a girl a bit older than he was, who seemed to know them, but he didn't know her.

"I've been waiting so long to meet you." The girl's smile widened even more. She had large hazel eyes and a sprinkling of freckles that ran across her nose and both cheeks. Her dark brown hair was loose and hung almost to her waist. It was straight until it curled up slightly at the ends. She had it tucked behind both ears.

"Since you don't know who I am, let me introduce myself," she said. "I'm Tay, Prince Robert's daughter and that makes me your cousin." At the word cousin, she shrieked a bit, clasped her hands together at her waist, and then dropped them to her sides.

"Our cousin?" Gabriella asked, smiling also. "Uncle Robert has kids?"

Holden watched the girl, Tay, smile back even brighter at Gabriella as she nodded in affirmation. Even though their uncle visited them quite a bit, their mom never allowed him to talk about himself very much or about where they came from. Holden knew that Gabby had always wanted more family and cousins. Now she had one right in front of her.

"A cousin," Holden said, slightly dismayed. Even though Gabby was excited, he wasn't sure he liked the idea of a cousin. He'd always enjoyed his uncle and spending time with him. If his uncle had kids, how much time would he want to spend with Holden here, in his land? This made him feel odd, a bit like he was losing his uncle.

"Yes." Tay continued to smile at them. "Come on, we need to get out of the bailey." She turned and walked toward the massive castle. Gabriella shrugged at Holden and followed. Holden shook his head, but followed also.

The sea of men garbed in green nudged their horses as they melted to the sides, parting for Tay. Many of the men gave simple nods as she passed. Tay nodded back to some but kept moving forward, leading the way for Gabby and Holden.

"Are there always this many men and so much activity?" Holden asked. Even though the movement of the men looked chaotic, he could see it really was not. They were gathering, meeting each other. Some were clasping each other's hands in greeting, and others were readying weapons. If he had to guess, they were in the beginning stages of preparation for an upcoming battle.

"Oh gosh no," Tay answered as she continued to move forward. "My grandfather, well, our grandfather that is, has sent out a call to arms. The army is gathering. Soon, there will be so many men, horses and equipment that they will have to start amassing outside of the castle."

"Really?" Holden smiled. It felt good to know that he'd been accurate.

"Yeah. That's why no one was there to meet you at the portal. My dad and his elite soldiers were dispatched to the borders of the Dark Kingdom. He only had a few minutes before he left and tasked me with watching for you to arrive."

Holden and Gabby both stopped and exchanged worried glances. They were supposed to meet their uncle in the Dark Kingdom.

"Why did Uncle Robert go to the Dark Kingdom?" Gabriella asked.

Tay looked at them, and then glanced around. Even though the men were respectful, they were still observant of their surroundings and watched closely what happened around them. "Let's talk inside."

Their cousin turned back around and led them toward the castle steps. Once there, she ran up them. Gabby and Holden did the same, keeping up with her.

Holden saw many of the men glancing at Gabby. They were looking at her scars. He would not have recognized them doing so if not for the way they reacted. After their initial glance, their gazes locked on her face. Soon after, surprise and dismay flitted across their features. He knew that her natural knee-jerk reaction was to put her head down and let her hair hide the scars that were visible on her cheek and neck. Yet she didn't. She held her head high and marched forward. When one of them looked too long, she gave him an equally long look in return. Holden felt proud of her, for not cowering and hiding what made her noticeably different from these people.

Her scars proved they weren't full leprechaun, but half human. Leprechauns had lifespans that lasted for thousands of years. The ability to heal fast was part of the reason they were able to live so long. Her scarring demonstrated to the men that their father was human.

"Don't let them bother you." Tay dropped into step next to Gabriella. The look she gave was full of understanding. Gabby self-consciously smoothed her hair over her cheek. Holden felt himself softening toward Tay, at the show of compassion she had just given his sister.

"My dad says there is more to someone than what we see, and these men don't know you," Tay told her.

"You don't really know me either," Gabriella said. She twisted her fingers into her soft, dark green skirt.

"I feel like I've known you for a very long time. Every time my dad went to visit you, he'd come home and tell me all about you and Holden. I really have been waiting ages to meet you," Tay said. She gave Gabriella another bright, warm smile, pulled Gabby's hands from her skirt and clasped them.

Gabriella smiled back at her, and returned the hand squeeze. "I wish I'd known about you."

"Me too," Tay responded.

Holden wanted to gag at the girly friendship that was blossoming. He rolled his eyes.

"Even though we are only half leprechaun." Gabriella's smile vanished.

Tay stopped walking and put her hand on her hips. "Even if you were half gargoyle or dragon," she said. Gabriella nearly ran into her, Tay had stopped walking so suddenly. Tay continued, "I don't care what the rest of them think. They believe themselves to be better, yet I don't. I'm happy to have you here, whatever you may be."

Holden was grateful for Tay's words. Although he felt somewhat ashamed to be half human—an assumption he made even though their mom wouldn't talk about or confirm it—he was proud too. He was a part of both worlds. It did frustrate him that the leprechauns didn't allow humans or human halflings to live in their realm. When he had more time, and after his mother was found safe, he wanted to question both his uncle and mother about this. The small taste he'd had of the leprechaun realm made him ache to stay or at least be able to visit more.

They arrived at the entrance to the castle. It opened up into a huge great hall, one that spanned at least eight stories in height. Two large stone staircases shot along either wall, and led to the upper floors. As they looked up, they saw the wide hall open to the landings and bannisters for each floor, all the way up to the clear glass ceiling. Many people traversed these walkways, going about their business. All were dressed in similar shades of green, with some creams, tans and brown leather footwear. In the middle of the hall were long wooden tables and benches. At least one hundred people could fit on each table and there were six of them. There was a seventh table, at the end and situated perpendicular to the other six. Giant fireplaces that stretched taller than a man's height dotted the walls on three sides. No fires were burning inside them at the moment. On either side, behind the table at the end, were two open archways that led to the back part of the castle.

"Woah," Holden said. He stopped and allowed the surroundings to soak in for a moment. The sheer size was intimidating.

"Yeah, woah," Gabriella echoed his sentiments and stilled her forward movement also. The place was massive. Holden didn't think he'd ever been inside somewhere so big and incredible before.

"I guess if you are not used to it, it might be a bit overwhelming," Tay said. She waved her hand in a circle to outline the castle laid out before them.

"Might be?" Gabriella said and looked at the upper floors. On all sides there were hallways that seemed to lead to inner rooms.

"Usually, there are not a lot of people in residence. The castle has really been filling up in the past hour, from the call to arms. We should get up to our private chambers before more arrive and we're in the way." Tay motioned for them to follow her as she hurried toward the first set of stairs on the left. As they passed by different people, some nodded and said nothing, while others nodded and addressed Tay as "mi-lady." Although they eyed Holden and Gabriella with curiosity, no one said anything or enquired as to who they might be. A few openly stared at Gabriella's scars.

After reaching the first set of stairs, the three children ran up them, then followed the long hall around the first landing until they came to the second set of stairs, which they ran up also. Following another long stretch of landing, they entered the door at the end, right before they would have turned to the second stretch of the landing. The door was a heavy wooden one, with a dark cherry color that contrasted well with the gray stone exterior. Tay easily pulled it open and stepped back to allow Gabriella and Holden through. Once they had entered, Tay followed them, before turning and shutting the door behind them.

Softer furnishings adorned the wide room. The stone walls were covered with different tapestries that hung from floor to ceiling and depicted many different scenes. One showed a battle of swordsmen upon horses, with rows of archers littered throughout, subduing a large gargoyle. Another showed a woman in a boat on a lake, reading from bound leaflets. Yet another showed a man bowing before a crowned man, while others looked on. Nearly all the subjects in the woven tapestries wore varied shades of green, while the outer trim of the tapestries was a darker hunter green.

Thick, dark wooden furniture, with green cushions had been spread throughout the room. Large, round pillows were haphazardly tossed about. They were similar in size, shape and color to large bean bags. Tay walked over to one and pulled it over to where two others were placed together. She plopped down in the middle of the one she had repositioned and motioned for Gabriella and Holden to do the same with the other two. They sat next to her.

"Why does everyone wear green here?" Holden asked, still studying the tapestries. He was especially interested in the ones depicting fighting scenes with gargoyles. He rested his hand on the top of his sword. After all the practicing he'd done with his uncle since he was old enough to properly hold a sword, he wanted to try it out in a real scenario. Of course, not one where anyone would be hurt, but he wanted to do something more than just swordplay. He also hoped to be able to try his hand at archery. Although he'd not brought his bow along, it was another activity that his uncle had coached him on and practiced with him when he would visit.

"That's the color of our house, our family," Tay said. "Our house rules the western lands, and the color is green. Each royal house has a certain color that they and their people wear."

"Why?" Holden looked from the tapestries to Tay.

"Well, I'm not sure exactly why. That's the way it's always been. I think it might have to do with the color of the land and the terrain mostly." Tay shrugged. It didn't seem to bother her that she didn't know why she had this custom.

"At home, we wear whatever color we want. Everybody does," Gabriella said. She ran her fingers over her skirt, smoothing it down over her knees.

"I like wearing green. I've never really thought about or wanted to wear something different. It's just the way it is here." Tay shrugged.

"It's strange. Everyone wearing the same color all the time. It's like wearing a uniform," Gabriella argued.

"These are my family's chambers," Tay said, waving her hands around the room as she changed the subject. "Your mom has chambers on the third floor, directly above these chambers. Although no one has been in residence since she left. That was before I was born."

"Really? Can we go see them?" Holden asked and clambered to his feet. As he stood, they all turned toward the sound of a knock at the chamber's door.

"Enter," Tay called out and pulled herself to a standing position. Gabriella did the same.

A woman with long brown hair plaited down her back and in similar dress and color entered. "Mi-lady," she gave a slight curtsy. "The king is requesting an immediate audience with you and your guests. He is in the council room." She nodded and then backed out the door, shutting it as she left.

"Uh oh," Tay said. She bit her bottom lip and chewed it back and forth. "My grandfather only holds an audience in the council room for important matters. I've never been called there before."

"Do you think it's because of us?" Holden asked.

"I don't know, it might be, or it could be related to the unexpected portal opening." Tay walked to the door. "We should go. Don't worry though. He is your grandfather too." She opened the door and motioned for them to follow.

# Chapter Eight

They followed Tay back down the stairs to the second level. She came to a chamber door and knocked once, then stood back and waited for someone to admit them. After a moment, the door was opened from the inside. The three of them entered an area much like the entrance to the chambers they had just left, although the insides of these chambers were very different. A large rectangular table stretched from one end of the room to the other. A few benches lined the table, but that was all. A large stone fireplace was in the back right corner, and guards stood at attention on each side of the chamber. They had on leather breast plates, with a large gargoyle stamped on the front, and their hands rested on their sheathed swords. They appeared ready for anything that might occur. There were no tapestries adorning the walls and only a few chairs were strewn about.

As they looked around, they noticed two taller, older gentlemen standing by the center of the table. One of the men looked up as the three entered. He said something they could not hear to the man standing next to him. The man gave the children a quick glance and then walked around the table, toward the children and the door. The exiting man was as tall as Uncle Robert, dressed in the same green clothing, and had gray streaking his brown hair. He took in Gabriella's scars and frowned but kept walking past them. His silent censure made Gabby lift her chin higher and look him in the eyes as he left.

The older man at the center table regarded them with a curious gaze. He wasn't dressed any different from the other men they had encountered. He had a sword at his hip, and wore green with gold-colored thread woven throughout. A resting gargoyle also crested his leather breastplate. He too had streaks of gray in his brown hair, but looked very much like Uncle Robert.

"Grandfather," Tay nodded her head in greeting. She walked up and stood opposite the man. Holden and Gabriella followed and stood on either side of her.

"Hello, Tay. Would you introduce me to your guests?" the man, their grandfather and the King of the Light Leprechauns, said.

Tay blushed and turned toward Gabby. "This is Gabriella." She then turned toward Holden. "This is Holden."

"Gabriella. Holden," the Light King said. His penetrating gaze made all three children a bit uncomfortable, especially the two newcomers.

"Hello," Gabriella said. Holden didn't say anything. He only stared up at his grandfather and studied him.

After a few more awkward moments, the Light King said, "This is a very bad time for a visit."

"Sorry," Gabriella mumbled. She wasn't sure what to say. This was the King of the Light Leprechauns, her mom's dad and her grandfather. He didn't look like what she expected a king to look like. He looked like the rest of the leprechauns and didn't wear a crown.

"We're not here for a visit." Holden refused to apologize. He stepped closer to the table.

"No?" The King straightened his shoulders more and returned Holden's challenging look.

"No. We're here to find our mom." Holden kept his chin high. He didn't care that this man was his grandfather or that he was the king.

"Holden, understand that I know that your mom is here, back in the realm. There is very little that I don't know. Yet I cannot and will not worry about your mom right now. I have other matters, more important, to attend to. When those are handled, the Light Leprechauns will find your mom. In the meantime, you children will need to stay in your mother's chambers here at the castle, out of the way. You will not go back to the human realm until your mother returns," the king spoke gently, but his manner was hard.

"But we are leprechauns too. We can help find our mom." Holden took a step forward.

The king lifted his hand. "Child, until it is determined exactly who you are; you will stay out of leprechaun affairs." The king looked at Gabriella as he said this. She flushed bright red. Holden knew she wanted to drop her head to hide her scars. Anger flushed his cheeks.

He opened his mouth to argue, but the king gave him a hard stare. He closed his mouth without saying anything. Gabriella looked at Holden, and her eyes willed him to stay silent. Holden had always had a really close relationship with their mom and at this moment, he missed her something fierce. He was used to the easy camaraderie he had with his uncle. This man standing before him was a stranger, keeping him from finding his mom. For a grandfather they had just met, to demand they listen to him, he was having a hard time remaining silent.

"Am I understood?" the king asked and looked from Holden to Gabby, before settling his gaze on Holden.

"Yes, sir," Gabriella answered immediately.

"Yes, I understand you," Holden answered slow and deliberate. He thinned his lips and lifted his chin higher.

"We will speak later. For now, you will go to your mother's chambers. Remain within the castle walls," the king ordered. He lifted his hand and gave a short wave toward the door. "Tay, show them to their quarters." the king motioned at his guards. The door opened and a large group of armed men entered.

"Yes, Grandfather," Tay responded with a slight nod.

"Come on," Tay said to Gabriella and Holden. She nodded at the guards as she passed them. Holden and Gabriella followed her lead, also nodding as they passed. The guards acknowledged them and returned their nods. Once they stepped out of the chamber, the door closed with a thud.

# CHAPTER NINE

Once the door closed behind them, Tay quickened her pace. In silence, she led them up the flight of stairs, back to her chambers. She pushed the door open and waited until they were all inside before she shut it hard behind her.

"Oh no, he was not happy at all." Tay frowned and tossed herself down on the large, overstuffed pillow she'd been lounging on earlier, before they'd been summoned to the king's common room.

Gabriella sank down next to her. "That was our grandfather," she said, to no one in particular. She wasn't sure how to feel. She'd always wanted to meet her mom's family but now that she'd met her grandfather, been admonished and dismissed, she felt odd. Her stomach had butterflies and she was a little sad.

Holden remained standing. "I'm not staying here," he said.

Tay and Gabby both looked up at him, surprised.

"You must. Grandfather ordered you to stay," Tay told him.

"I don't care," Holden said.

"You have to care, he's the king," Tay said.

"He's not my king." Holden walked over to the window to look out.

"Yes, he is. You're his grandson, so he is definitely your king," Tay crossed her arms over her chest. "And besides, you can't go anywhere anyways."

"Why not?" Holden was still looking out the window.

"The castle is full of soldiers preparing for battle," Tay said.

"There's got to be a way out. We were let in easy enough."

"You were let in easy because I was waiting for you," Tay said. "Without me there, you would have been taken inside to the barracks to be questioned until it was determined what was to be done with you. I made it easy."

"I bet you know a way out." Holden turned to look at her.

Tay refused to answer him. She sat with her arms still folded across her chest, staring at him. Her chin was set at a stubborn angle, much like his was.

"Holden, leave her alone," Gabriella told him.

"Gabby, don't you want to find mom?" Holden asked her.

"Well, of course I do," she said. "I want to leave right now and go to the Dark Castle, but how can we after our grandfather ordered us to stay here?"

"The Dark Castle!" Tay exclaimed and dropped her arms. She sat up straight and looked at Gabby. "What do you mean go to the Dark Castle? You can't go there!"

"Uncle Robert, I mean, your dad, thinks our mom is being held there," Holden said.

"We're supposed to go there and he was going to meet us to help get her," said Gabby.

"Oh no. He didn't tell me that part." Tay slumped back down in her cushion. "This is bad, really bad."

"Why's it so bad?" Gabriella leaned forward.

"The huge portal that was opened, it was opened in the Dark Kingdom," Tay said. "The army is preparing to march there to close it. The other High Kings are preparing their armies too, to meet our army there. You can't go to the Dark Kingdom. All three armies of the High Kingdoms will be there."

"Then we have to get our mother," Gabriella said. "If a bunch of armies are marching there, we've got to get her before any armies arrive."

"You don't understand. The portal that's been opened is huge, one of the largest since the battle with humans thousands of years ago," Tay explained. "This type of portal takes many leprechauns to open. The Dark King must have pulled together his most powerful alchemists to open it. This goes against the treaty with the humans, to protect their world and keep creatures from other realms out."

"I knew there was a treaty, but my mom spoke very little of it, other than to say one existed." Holden sat down with the girls.

"A few thousand years ago, when the High Kings were very young, many portals to the human realm were open. Creatures from other worlds traveled in and out of the human world. Leprechauns didn't really pay attention to the human realm much, until minor leprechauns began disappearing. The humans had learned how to capture the females and began taking them. They forced them to close portals and create gold. It sparked a war. After many, many years and battles where both sides took heavy losses, the human and leprechaun kings came to an agreement. The leprechauns would close the portals to the human realm and protect any portals that were kept open between worlds. They would also keep creatures from other realms from entering the human world, and also never interfere in human affairs. In return, the humans would have nothing to do with leprechauns or any other realm and keep to themselves. This was hard for some leprechauns. A few humans and leprechauns also intermarried, but the humans had very short lives. Those leprechauns were allowed to stay amongst the humans, but forbidden to reveal their leprechaun nature. Living there was frowned upon though, and very few leprechauns stayed in the human world. Once the war was over, most returned to the leprechaun realm. When your mom left to go live in the human world, it shocked everyone."

"I don't understand. I thought leprechauns were more powerful than humans. How did they not win all the battles?" Holden asked. He sat with his knees pulled up to his chest, his arms wrapped around them.

"Leprechauns are more powerful than humans, but they live for a very long time and there aren't as many. There are hundreds of humans to every one leprechaun. They far outnumber us, and because of that, the sheer numbers make up a formidable force," Tay said. "Plus, it all depends on how powerful the leprechaun is. A minor leprechaun with very little abilities is not as powerful as a royal leprechaun."

"How many High Kings are there and why are they called High Kings?" Gabriella asked. She fingered her skirt. It was a soft, thick linen and the gold threads at the hems glistened as she turned the fabric.

"There are three High Kings and they come from the three parts of the leprechaun realm: the Light, the Dark and the Ash. They are High Kings because they each hail from the most powerful of the royal families. They are the strongest leprechauns. The three of them get together once a year to discuss matters important to the leprechauns. Although the Dark King no longer attends. Not since the battle with the humans. He did not agree with the treaty, but the other two kings did."

"The Light Kingdom, this one we are from," Tay continued, "has lands that stretch all the way from the sea up to the high mountains. Our weather is milder and the sun shines quite a bit here." Tay grinned proudly at this. Her bright smile made her eyes gleam. "The high mountains are the territory of the Dark Kingdom. It is cold most of the time, with steep mountains and deep valleys. The colors of that Kingdom are black and red. The Ash Kingdom is the Kingdom of the sea and the islands through the sea. Their colors are gray and blue."

"Why doesn't our grandfather want us to leave the castle?" Gabriella asked. If her grandfather had more important matters to attend, then it didn't seem like it would matter what they did.

"Well, there are a few reasons, but the main one is because we are young. I don't have any abilities yet, and am not sure if you two will get them." She frowned when she said this.

"Because we're half human," Gabriella finished for her. "It's okay. Don't worry about offending us. We understand." Gabby sighed. "I never really thought too much about being half human or half leprechaun until we came here. Now, it seems a little unfair." It was probably one of the reasons their mom was raising them in the human world, so they were not looked down upon.

"Yeah, it does," Holden agreed with his sister.

"Don't worry about it though. I'm glad you're here, no matter what," Tay said in an attempt to make them feel better.

"Even though we are young and don't have abilities, why should that matter?" Holden argued. "We're not planning on doing anything special. We just need to make it to the Dark Kingdom."

"Leprechaun children are always escorted and have constant protection." Tay looked at Holden like he'd grown two heads. "Didn't your mom ever explain that to you?"

"No," Holden answered. Gabby nodded in agreement with Holden.

"And my dad didn't either?" Tay seemed surprised.

"No, when your dad visited, we talked about school, how we were doing. Then we would practice, swords or archery. Don't get me wrong, I loved to practice with him, but he didn't talk very much."

Tay shook her head. "That sounds like my dad. Leprechaun boys practice archery and swordsmanship daily until they are old enough and start getting their abilities. They need to have their skills honed before then."

"I've noticed that all the men around here carry swords, but I haven't seen many bows," Holden said. He rested his chin on his knees. "On the arriving horsemen, I saw a few, but everyone had swords."

"Bows are used for battle and when the men are beyond the castle gates," Tay told him.

"Ah, that makes sense," Holden responded. "Yet it still doesn't answer my question. Why does it matter if we are children, without protection and unescorted?"

"Because you'd be vulnerable to anyone and anything," she said. "It might be the leprechaun realm, with three kingdoms to protect it, but anything can happen.

Sometimes creatures and other beings make it through portals. They don't usually bother leprechauns, because they know the dangers of doing so. Yet children don't have the ability to protect themselves and are as vulnerable as humans. Leprechaun children are highly valued by their parents, as there is usually only one or two kids per family. It is very rare for leprechauns to have more than two children. Some may not even have children for a thousand years or more."

Holden stiffened and sat up. "I can protect myself just fine," he boasted.

Tay laughed. "I'm sure you think you can, but you really can't."

"It doesn't matter. I'm not staying here. I'm going after my mother. Uncle Robert said he'd meet us there, and even if he can't, I'm still going."

"That's impossible!" Tay got to her knees, facing Holden. "You can't leave."

"Tay," Gabriella broke into the conversation. "Holden's right. We can't stay. It's our mom."

"But, you don't understand. It's too dangerous and grandfather ordered you to stay." She tried to make them see reason. Her grandfather gave a direct order, and as High King of their people, his orders were to be obeyed. "Plus, you don't even know where you're going."

"You could tell us," Gabriella pleaded with her. She got to her knees and looked Tay directly in the eyes. "You could help us. Please?"

"I . . . I . . . I'd get into so much trouble." Tay was afraid of helping, but also knew she'd feel the same way if it were her mom or dad. She wished her mother was here right now. She was in the neighboring village, or she would be having this conversation with Holden and Gabby.

"Tay, please. I know we only just met you, but we must go. We really can't stay here while our mom is being held. What if something happens to her?" Holden said.

"What if something happened to you? Have you thought of that?" Tay shot back.

"Then something happens. But we can't just sit here." Holden stood and lifted his backpack, then slung it over his shoulders. He tapped his sword, ensuring it was in place. "I'm going. You can help us or not."

Gabriella stood also. She slung her backpack over her shoulders, and nodded. "Me too. I would love to stay, to see our mom's chambers, but not now. Maybe later, once our mom is safe."

Tay stood and faced them. "Do you know what you are asking of me?" she asked.

"To help us," Holden said.

"You are asking me to commit treason," Tay said softly. "To go against my king."

"But he's our grandfather," Gabriella said.

"It doesn't matter. He's still my king. He gave me an order." Tay let her head fall.

Holden's shoulders slumped. Without her help, getting out of the castle would be hard. He didn't know the layout or the men. Gabriella hadn't practiced sword fighting during their uncle's visits. She'd talk and laugh with him, but she never trained much at all. In a fight, she would be little help.

"I'll help you," Tay whispered.

"You will?" Gabriella and Holden said at the same time.

"Yes." Tay looked back up at them. "I shouldn't but I will."

"Awesome. Thanks so much," Gabriella said.

"We'll make it up to you somehow, Tay," Holden told her.

"Yeah, you will. You'll come back safe and stay, so I can get to know you better and not just through stories my dad has told me." She looked at them. Hard. "Agreed?"

"Agreed," Holden and Gabriella echoed.

Tay squared her shoulders. "Let's get you my father's bow and get out of here," she told Holden. "I'll return soon. Wait here."

# CHAPTER TEN

A rapid knock at the chamber door startled them. Tay had just taken a step toward the door, intent on retrieving her father's bow. The knock stopped her. All three children looked at each other, but it was Tay's eyes that widened the most.

"I'm not expecting anyone, yet with your recent arrival, it could be anyone," she said, her voice wavering as she moved across the room.

"I'm nervous and on the verge of deceiving the family and clan I've known my entire life, and someone decides to knock on the door. Great. Just great," she muttered while she walked.

Another knock sounded at the chamber door, echoing throughout the chamber. Tay strode faster to the door and wrenched it open. Her frustration quickly turned to surprise.

"Ann!" Tay exclaimed.

It was one of her father's sentries, one who had been posted somewhere other than the castle for quite some time. Tay didn't know where, she only knew it was not at the castle. To have her standing before her now was a bit of a shock.

Holden looked at the woman standing in front of Tay. She was of average height, with medium length black hair. She was clad in a long, dark green unadorned dress with plain cream lacing in the front. Her hair was partially pulled up near her temples and the back fell in loose ringlets down a bit past her shoulders. The strands that hung loose vacillated between shades of stark, dark black and bright, royal blue. Even though she was dressed in green, the blue didn't clash; it blended well with the color of her bright blue eyes.

"Tay." Ann gave Tay a quick nod of greeting, then stepped around her, entering the chamber. She pulled the door closed behind her. Tay's mouth opened in surprise at Ann's bold affront, but she shut it almost immediately. Not before Ann noticed, however.

"When did you return?" Tay demanded as she followed Ann to where Holden and Gabriella sat watching their interaction, quiet.

"Wouldn't you like to know?" Ann grinned and winked at Tay.

"Ann!" Tay tilted her head and tossed her hands in the air in exasperation. She let them fall back at her sides. "Seriously. You've been gone, what, almost two years?"

"Yep," Ann quipped back at her, still smiling. Holden could see that Ann liked Tay and enjoyed teasing her for the reaction.

"All sentries and outposts have been recalled to the castle." Ann's grin faded and her expression turned more serious.

"All? Recalled?" Tay was surprised at this. Never in her life had this happened. "Even you?"

"Yes, even me, midget." Ann's serious expression lightened for a brief moment as she flashed a quick smile at Tay. "I'll be joining your father's ranks shortly, but wanted to meet these two first." She nodded at Gabriella and Holden.

"Um, hello." Gabriella stood and stuck her hand out in introduction.

Ann frowned at Gabriella's hand, then tossed back her head and laughed.

Gabriella almost let her hand drop when Ann seized it and lifted it high above her head. Gabby yelped as Ann then snatched her other hand and lifted it high also, holding both of her hands aloft in a V shape. Holden tensed and swung his feet around.

"Hasn't your mother taught you anything? Or your uncle, for that matter?" Ann sneered at Gabriella, holding her hands high and outstretched.

"What are you doing?" Tay stepped around Ann and tried to pull down Gabby's arms.

"Step back, Tay," Ann ordered, her voice serious and strong and not allowing for further argument. Tay dropped her hands to her sides and stepped back, her brow creased. Holden had seen enough. If Tay was worried, something was wrong. He pulled out his little dagger and jumped to his feet. He moved fast and in a few steps, he had his dagger at the woman's back.

Ann must have felt the dagger pressing into her back because she chuckled. Despite the laugh, she didn't release Gabriella. Ann kept Gabby's arms raised and pulled apart. Gabriella was struggling and glaring, but Ann was taller and much stronger.

"Let my sister go. Now," Holden said, quiet but assured. With his feet planted firmly, he stood directly behind her. The tip of his dagger was poking against the bottom of her back.

"Very good, little Prince." Ann lowered Gabriella's hand and spun around to face Holden. She knocked the dagger from his hands and it clattered across the chamber floor, coming to rest next to a dark mahogany chest.

Holden sucked in a breath. He put his hand at his sword, prepared to draw. Although he wasn't sure who this new leprechaun woman was, it didn't matter. Even if she was one of his uncle's sentries. His uncle had failed to meet them here. She had just grabbed Gabriella. That made her an immediate foe. He needed to defend his sister.

"You grabbed my sister," Holden said.

"Of course I did, little Prince." Ann gave him a wry grin. "The young princess offered her hand, her most precious gift and weapon," Ann told him, tilting her head at Gabriella.

"My hand?" Gabriella lifted the hand she had offered to Ann. "It was a handshake. I was offering you a handshake, nothing else." She took a step back and rubbed her arms.

"Oh yeah, Gabby." Tay let out a deep breath and Holden observed recognition of the grave error dawn across her features. "A female leprechaun's power is centered in her hands. They never willingly touch hands with others."

"Princess, we don't shake hands," Ann told Gabriella, quite firm. "Don't ever offer your hand to another."

"I'm not a princess." Gabriella shook her head at Ann.

"Is your mother not the daughter of the king? Are you not her daughter?" she raised her eyebrows as she asked Gabriella the question. She turned her head to Holden. "Are you not her son?"

Holden didn't respond. He only looked at her, his hand still on his sword. She might be baiting them, trying to get them to answer for a reason. He wasn't going to say anything.

"We are, but we are not full leprechaun, so we aren't anything," Gabby answered instead.

"Huh," Ann grunted. "Not anything," she said and looked between them.

"They're half human," Tay offered in explanation.

"Really?" Ann asked, still not looking convinced. "Is that so?"

"Yeah," Gabriella confirmed. "Our dad was human."

Ann gave her a hard stare, then looked at Holden, not saying anything for a few moments. He frowned at her. He wanted to shout at her to leave them alone or at least shift his feet but he stood still and returned Ann's gaze.

"Alright then," Ann finally broke the eye contact and looked at Tay. "You children stay here, no matter what happens." She looked back at Gabriella. "I'll return when I am able. You have a lot to learn, Princess." A wry smirk accompanied the last word. She gave a quick wink to Holden, turned around, and let herself out of the chamber, closing the door quietly behind her.

"What in the world was that?" Gabriella asked Tay.

Tay started laughing. "That," she said, "was Ann." She kept laughing. "That's my dad's favorite sentry. She has a strong spirit and is a colorful character. Few ever cross her. You never know what to expect with Ann."

"I guess not." Gabriella shook her head slowly and a smile appeared.

Holden didn't laugh or smile like his sister and cousin. He didn't find the situation as funny as they appeared too.

"Tay," Holden interrupted, "maybe we should go now? I don't like how everyone keeps telling us to stay." He felt even more like a prisoner and wanted to get going, on their way to finding their mom and hopefully at some point, uncle.

"I don't know, you guys. Ann just said we should stay also," Tay said, frowning.

"Please, Tay," Gabriella pleaded. "We want to find our mom."

Tay's shoulders fell a bit. "You have a good point," she said. "Your mom is out there and I don't know when my dad will be able to help her. Alright, let me gather a few items from my dad's room, then we'll go."

# CHAPTER ELEVEN

After Tay had gone into her father's room and returned with two bows, two quivers full of arrows, and two thick black capes, she led them out of the chambers and the castle. There was so much activity in the castle they were able to pass quickly and without much notice.

As they walked, Tay explained more about their destination. "We're going to the portal that will transport you to the border village," she said, speaking fast and in a hushed voice.

It was where leprechauns, both Dark and Light, lived and mixed on the edge of the border between the two kingdoms. Although it was frowned upon, there were some who did live together. From the border village, Holden and Gabriella could purchase horses with the extra bow and quiver of arrows. Then they were to follow the trail up into the mountains. It would wind up to the Dark Castle. From there, they'd be on their own. As soon as her father returned, she'd tell him where they'd gone and send him along as fast as possible.

"Although I don't know when he's coming back. There might not be any help for a very long time," she told them as they walked under the ramparts on the north side of the castle's perimeter walls.

"We'll be okay," Holden said.

Gabriella wasn't so sure. As courageous as she was trying to be, she was scared. This place wasn't like home. Nevertheless, she said, "Yeah, we will be fine." She was feeling hot too. Her hands were itchy and sweaty and her scars were throbbing. She wasn't sure why she was feeling this way again, but it was bothering her. It wasn't the time to feel bad, not when she was about to set out on one of the most frightening trips of her life.

"Remember, when we get to the portal, smile and laugh. Hug me and thank me for my hospitality. Don't act worried. The guards will sense right away if something is wrong. Also, have you gone through many portals?" she asked.

"Just two," Holden said, holding up two fingers.

"One at the witch's bookshop and one at the goblins' house," Gabriella added.

"Did they have doors that covered them, or were they open portals?"

Gabriella and Holden looked at each other for a moment. The witch had opened a door and the goblins had opened a door also. "I think they had doors covering them. Doors were opened before we stepped through," Gabriella said.

"Ok, some portals are like that. This one isn't. It's an open portal. It will have a perimeter of gold and look like whatever it is opened against. It was opened on the castle wall, to allow quicker travel to the borderland village. It's guarded on this side, as it's a two-way portal. You can travel back and forth through it. It looks like a stone wall, but it's a portal. Don't hesitate. Just walk right through. You won't hit a wall. I promise." Tay smiled as she told them this.

"The one you entered to get from the goblins to here is only one way, and only comes from the king's goblin advisors. It is rarely guarded, as that is the job of the goblins on the other side," Tay said as they continued to walk along the castle walls. They were keeping to the inside of the wall, to avoid the chaos and commotion, and also the notice of the gathering army.

"The king has goblin advisors?" Gabriella asked.

"Yes. They advise him on matters outside the realm of the leprechauns," Tay answered. She lifted her skirt and stepped gingerly over a few flowers that were growing wild next to the castle walls.

"So, the ones we met were the advisors or the guards of the portal?" Gabriella asked.

"What were their names? Do you know what they were called?" Tay asked her.

"Bentley and Gildseth," Holden said.

"Ah, yes. Bentley and Gildseth. They are the advisors and guards. I don't like them. They are always so serious, they come for a quick visit, speak with the king and leave just as quickly as they came." Tay frowned. "They allowed you through the portal?"

"Yes. The witch told us to give them payment and we did." Gabriella shrugged.

"Huh. That's interesting. No one ever comes through the portal but them, or sometimes my dad," Tay observed.

They approached a large outbuilding. On the left side were two armed men, standing next to part of the castle wall that was behind the outbuilding. There was a thick gold square etched in the wall, and each man stood on either side of it. The men looked at them curiously, but remained silent.

"Hello Toth. Adam." Tay smiled as she sauntered up to them.

"Your highness." They both gave her a quick nod. Tay gave them a short nod in return.

"I'm escorting Miranda and Stephen back home. Well, of course not all the way back. Their parents should be on the other side." Tay let out a small laugh that came out as a tinny tinkle. Gabby resisted the urge to cringe. Her cousin wasn't a very good actor.

The one Tay had addressed as Toth looked down at them, skepticism etched across his facial features. "Your highness, we've had no orders to allow anyone through."

Tay put her hands on her hips. "What? How are they supposed to get home?" She frowned up at the tall guard.

"My dad would be here, but as you know, he has more important matters he's busy with right now." Tay lifted her right hand from her hip and waved it in the air, frustrated.

Toth shifted his stance. He looked at the other guard. Adam shrugged. Tay did have a point.

"Do you want me to go back inside the castle and get my grandfather just to let them go home?" Tay asked, incredulous. She half turned, intent on marching back to the castle. "Fine. I will. But don't get upset at me when grandfather is angry for this little interruption. Believe me, I'd rather have Miranda and Stephen stay a few more days, but their parents are expecting them. Think of the mess if they don't show up." Tay threw both hands in the air this time. "It won't be my fault."

"Not to worry, your highness. We'll allow them through. Don't bother the king. He has very important issues to deal with." Adam stepped aside and Toth followed his lead.

Tay turned to Holden and Gabriella. She nodded at them and said in a formal manner, "Thank you for visiting. Please visit again soon."

Gabriella stepped forward, nodded to Tay, then stepped to the portal. Holden watched her, worried that she'd walk straight into a stone wall, but he was more worried of what was on the other side. Something unknown and dangerous. He watched warily as his sister stepped through.

She disappeared with ease. It was amazing. One second Gabriella was there, and the next, she was gone, into the stone wall. The gold shimmered as she went through.

Holden turned to his cousin Tay.

"Goodbye," he said, mimicking the formality they were observing.

Tay ignored the formality and dropped the act for a moment. She tossed her arms around Holden's waist and gave him a quick hug. Holden stood in shock for a few seconds, before uncomfortably returning the hug.

"Be careful," Tay whispered in his ear, then stepped back.

He rested his right hand on his sword, gripped tight the bow he had slung on his other shoulder, and followed his sister through the portal.

# CHAPTER TWELVE

"Holden." Gabriella grabbed her brother's hand and hauled him forward. All around them people walked, going about their day. Some pushed small carts, filled with vegetables and other wares, while others carried baskets and wooden crates. It was a large open market they had stepped into.

Gabriella turned and looked behind them. The portal they had stepped through was on the side of a large wooden building. It appeared to be a one-way portal, like the one they had entered from the goblins' realm. She had expected to see guards or soldiers guarding the portal, but there were none. And for the most part, people ignored them. It might be the case that, the portal being hidden and guarded on the other side, there was no need for extra security on this side.

When she had stepped through the portal, her hands itched. She opened and closed them a few times. Her scars were itching and pulsing too. Something about the shimmering gold affected her. Ignoring the itchy, warm feeling in her hands and on the side of her face, she looked around.

All along their side of the market, she saw wooden houses, with wooden decks that connected them. They appeared to be store fronts, having stalls to display their wares, yet they lacked windows to whatever was inside.

"Where should we go?" Gabriella looked at Holden. He was glancing around, taking in his surroundings.

"I'm not sure. Maybe we should just walk around," Holden said. He stepped out onto the dirt street and toward the stall vendors.

They walked to the right. Goods of all types were being sold, from fruit and vegetables to clothing, in shades of green, black and crimson, and blue and gray. Gabriella stepped up to one of the clothing stalls and fingered a linen dress of gray.

"Going to the Ash Kingdom?" An older woman dressed in black and crimson stepped forward. She had long brown hair, streaked with gray and tied back in a bun, yet her face had very few wrinkles.

"No, I'm just looking," Gabriella said.

"Few people just look, child. Most have a purpose," the woman replied, looking them over.

"We do have a purpose. Yet my sister wanted to look at clothes." Holden stepped forward to defend his sister.

The woman laughed at the young boy standing before her. "Then a purpose you have."

"Yes," Gabriella and Holden said at the same time.

"Our purpose is to get horses for travel. Where would we find those?" Holden asked.

The woman's smile disappeared and crease lines appeared around her mouth in a small frown. "Where are your parents? Surely you children are not travelling alone."

"No, we're not alone," Gabriella answered quickly. "Our parents are getting other supplies. We are to find horses."

"Hmmm . . ." The older woman continued to study them. After a few uncomfortable moments, she pointed toward the end of the street market. "There, down at the end, you will find stables. They will help you with the horses you seek."

"Thank you," Gabriella said, and gave a quick nod of thanks. Nodding seemed to be the proper thing to do in the leprechaun realm. She noticed that nearly everyone nodded at the end or beginning of a conversation or when first meeting. The older woman gave her a nod in return. Gabriella and Holden quickly scurried away.

"I think we should try not to talk to many people," Gabriella said as they walked down the street.

"Yeah, that was uncomfortable," Holden agreed. He hoisted the bow over his shoulder and rearranged it. It was larger than the one he used at home and was not sitting well across his shoulder and chest.

"Which bow are we keeping and which are we trading?" Gabriella asked Holden, watching him readjust as they walked.

"How about we trade the one you're carrying?" Holden said. "I'll keep this one, just in case."

"Sounds good," Gabriella said.

They came to the end of the street, where a large barn-like building stood. Next to it were many corrals, containing horses of all colors and sizes. They stepped inside the big open doorway and looked around for someone to help them. Stalls lined either side of the barn. A man dressed in brown leather boots, brown breeches and a green tunic walked toward them from the back of the stables.

"Hello. Welcome," he said in greeting. He had a large smile on his face and they instantly relaxed in his company. "I'm the stable master. How may I help you?"

"We need two horses," Holden said.

"You need two horses?" The man asked, his smile dimming a bit.

"Yes," Gabriella said. "We have this to trade," she dropped her left shoulder and let the bow slide off. She held it forward for the man to inspect.

"This nice bow, in trade for two horses?" the man asked her, seeming incredulous.

"Yes, this is all we have to trade," Gabriella told him. "We will need saddles and anything else required for travel also."

"May I ask, where are your parents?"

"They are gathering the other supplies needed for our trip. We were tasked with getting the horses," she told him.

"They're fine with you trading such a nice bow for the horses?" the man pressed. He seemed uneasy about taking the bow in trade.

"They told us to trade it. It is our main item of value and we really need horses," Gabriella explained. She hoped that he would not see through their farce and demand to wait for their parents to show up.

"Very well. I will bring you my two finest horses and all the tack you will need." He set the bow against the stable closest to him before walking away. Gabriella stepped over and set the quiver of arrows she had with it. The man had not asked about them, but she figured that they went together.

"It's strange how they keep asking where our parents are," Holden told her.

"Yeah, but you heard Tay explain how leprechaun children are never alone. It really must be an unusual thing for us to be out here by ourselves," she replied.

"We need to get the horses and get out of here fast," said Holden.

"Yeah," Gabriella agreed. "We'll ride out of here right away, then once we're far enough from everyone, we can stop and figure out exactly where we need to go."

"Good idea, Gabby. That way, no one else can ask us where our parents are." Holden readjusted his bow across his shoulders again. It really was too big for him.

"Want me to carry that now?" Gabriella offered.

"No, I got it." Even though it was a bigger bow than Holden was used to, it felt good to have the weapon, along with his sword. Just in case of anything happening or needing to defend themselves. Half of him hoped nothing would happen, but the other half was curious to see how well he would do. To see how much his training with his uncle had taught him.

They waited in silence and looked around at their surroundings. At first glance, the barn had looked simple, but upon closer inspection, it was anything but. Each of the stable doors was polished smooth, with no rough wooden edges. Someone had meticulously carved scroll patterns on each of the doors and inlaid them with small, golden decorations that resembled runes of some sort. There was very little metal on the doors, and nearly all had carved wooden hinges instead of metal.

The stable master came back into the barn, leading two horses. One was white, with brown patches all over and a brown mane and tail. The other was jet black, with four white socks and a white blaze down the front of its face. They were both saddled, with brown leather saddles and green blankets under the saddles. They appeared ready to go. Dark green bedrolls were tied on their backs, at the end of the saddles. The saddles were tooled leather and lacked horns, much like the English style of saddles back home, in the human realm.

"Besides the two horses, does your party need anything else?" The stable master asked them, holding the horses.

"No, we have everything else we need," Gabriella replied.

"Are you sure you're not wanting to stay the night? It's going to be dark soon," he said, reluctant to hand over the horses.

Gabriella and Holden looked at each other. They hadn't considered traveling in the dark.

"We'll be fine," Gabriella replied slowly. "We really need to get on our way. Our parents are waiting for us, and we must set out soon."

"Well then. Here you go." The stable master handed each of them a set of reins. Gabriella took the brown and white horse, while Holden took the black one. In unison, they each slipped a foot in the stirrup on the left of their horses, stood and tossed a leg over. Gabriella's long dress flipped up a bit, but she quickly tucked it around her legs until only her leather boots were revealed as far as her calves.

At that moment, Gabriella was happy that Uncle Robert had insisted on taking them riding at the local stables during many of his visits. She felt comfortable and confident on top of a horse and was glad that it showed. She pulled down and back at the reins with a light touch and her horse backed up a few steps.

Holden took a moment more to settle. He adjusted his sword and bow until he was comfortable with both. Then he looked at Gabby, to see if she was ready. She smiled at him, then nodded at the bow and the quiver, propped against a stable door.

"Your payment, sir," she told the stable master and gave him a nod. Holden nodded also. The stable master nodded back.

"Good luck to you," he said as they nudged their horses forward. They rode out of the stables and onto the main road. From there, they took a left and headed out of the bustling village. It took ten more minutes to reach the outskirts because they had to dodge people walking in front of and beside them.

# CHAPTER THIRTEEN

Once they left the outskirts of the village, they kicked their horses into a gallop. They rode for about ten more minutes at the quickened pace before Holden signaled Gabriella to hold up.

She slowed her horse to a walk and pulled alongside Holden. "That was fun," she said.

"Yeah, I love galloping and there is so much more room here, instead of at the arena back home." He grinned at her. Then his expression became somber. He pointed toward the looming mountains. "This seems to be the only road, so I'm guessing we take this one."

Gabriella's gaze followed his arm. The mountains were gorgeous and imposing. Snow lined many of the peaks, and a lush expanse of evergreen trees wound their way around them. She looked from the mountains to the sun, which was getting lower in the sky.

"Should we ride for a bit longer, then find somewhere to make camp?" she asked.

"Yeah. Maybe we gallop for a while longer, to get as far away from here as possible. That way, when we stop, the horses can rest and we can sleep."

"Um, Holden, do you think it's safe to camp here?" Gabriella asked. "Tay said that many different creatures live here too."

"What if one of us sleeps while the other one stands guard?" Holden asked. "That way, nothing can sneak up on us while we sleep."

"Good idea," Gabriella said. "Come on, let's try to get as far as we can tonight." She kicked her horse back into a gallop and Holden did the same. After a few moments, they were pounding down the narrow dirt road, heading toward the mountains. The ground began to slope gradually as they began their ascent and the horses slowed a bit to compensate for the terrain. More and more trees began to line the road. After a while, not more than an hour, the setting sun began to cast long shadows from the trees. They continued to ride until the sun had almost dipped beyond the horizon and just a bit of light was left. A half moon rose in the distance, off to their right. Stars blinked on in the sky. They slowed the horses to a walk and began to glance around, looking for a good place to stop and make camp.

"Do you think we should ride into the trees, or stay next to the road?" Gabriella asked.

"I'd kinda like to stay next to the road, but maybe in a few trees, so that if someone was coming down the road, they wouldn't see us," Holden answered.

"I agree. But I don't want to go in too far. We don't know what's in there." Gabriella shivered a little. It wasn't just the thought of the unknown that had her shivering. With the setting sun, the air had chilled.

"Let's go over here." Holden led his horse toward an opening in the trees. He ducked under a branch and went around a tree. Gabriella followed , mimicking his motions as they picked their way through the trees. After they'd gone in about five trees deep, the tree line opened to reveal a small meadow. Holden dismounted and pulled his reins over the horse's head. His horse shook his head, while Holden stretched his back.

Gabriella dismounted also, pulled her reins over her horse's head. She stretched too. Although it had felt good to ride, it felt better to stand on solid ground. She walked her horse over to the closest tree and tied one loose end of the rein to the low tree branch. She pulled it tight to test it, then let the loose end drop. Knowing the horse was secure, she walked the few steps to the back of the saddle and began untying her bedroll. She turned to find that Holden had already tied his horse to the tree next to hers, untied his bedroll and was walking into the meadow. After a few more steps, bringing him closer to the center of the small meadow, he tossed his bedroll on the ground along with his backpack, bow and quiver. He kept his sword buckled.

Gabriella followed him, squinting in the disappearing light. She thought she could see the trail they had just come from wind up the mountain. This seemed like a good spot. If anyone came down the mountain, they might possibly see them first.

"Why don't you try to get some sleep first?" Gabriella told Holden.

"Are you sure? I can stay awake for a while longer." Holden shrugged off his backpack, let it drop and sat on his bedroll.

"I'm sure. You get some sleep first," she said.

Gabriella tossed her bedroll next to Holden, shrugged off her backpack too, let it drop and plopped down. She opened her backpack and pulled out the black and crimson cape.

"Aha! A blanket," She shook it out. Holden laughed, finding one in his pack as well.

"Good idea," he said as he lay down and covered up with his.

Gabriella pulled a roll of Ritz crackers from her backpack. She ripped open the package and handed Holden a few. He didn't sit up, but stuffed the crackers in his mouth and chewed them lying down. It had been an extremely long day for both of them. She ate a few crackers herself, but remained sitting. Then she twisted the end of the package and put it back into her bag. She looked over to her brother. His eyes were closed, even though he was still chewing.

"Holden, are you really going to sleep with your sword on?" Gabriella asked.

Holden opened his eyes and sat up. He unbuckled his sword belt and lay it between them. "There, just in case you need it while I'm sleeping," he told her. Then he lay back down and closed his eyes. Within a few minutes, he was breathing softly, fast asleep.

Gabriella lay down next to him. She intended to keep watch, but she didn't see a reason why she couldn't lay down for a little while. After a few minutes, she was fast asleep.

# CHAPTER FOURTEEN

Gabriella heard the whisper, soft, yet quite urgent, like a man hollering at her through ten layers of sleeping bags.

"Wake up, child. Wake up, Gabriella," the man urged. He had a deep, rich timbre to his voice.

She mumbled in her sleep, "No."

"Wake up, put your hands together and bring me home," he cajoled.

Gabriella shifted in her sleep, but did not fully wake up. She was at that point between consciousness and waking, when dreams were possible, but at the fringe. Her face was hot and her hands even hotter.

"Feel the heat, child. Let the heat flow," the man said. Something shrieked, loud and fierce in the background of his words. "Put your hands together and let the heat flow."

Her hands were on fire and her face felt as if molten lava was streaking all along her scars. She whimpered and shifted, then rolled on her side. This wasn't her first dream like this. She'd been having similar dreams for a few weeks now.

"That's it. Wake up. Put your hands together and let the heat meet within your hands," the man's plea became more serious, desperate. More shrieks, like from a wild animal, sounded behind him. "Do it. Do it now!"

Gabriella sat up, not quite awake. The heat was nearly unbearable. The scars on the side of her face burned furiously. The urge to join her hands grew intolerable. She gave in to the compulsion and clasped her hands together. Light exploded from them as heat burst forth. The action jolted her into awareness. Startled completely awake, she looked down at her hands and the brilliant colors erupting from them. Shimmers of gold wavered before her, dancing from her hands.

"Now pull. Pull them apart and create a door for me," the man's voice was distant now, almost imperceptible.

Gabriella began to pull her hands apart and felt a tugging from within the core of her. It was like that feeling you had when you were throwing up, over and over again from an awful bout with the flu. It felt like her guts were twisting. The liquid gold shimmered and the colors became more vibrant, sending a brilliant rainbow straight up into the sky that had already lightened from night to day. She moved her hands farther apart and the gold elongated into a shimmering horizontal line.

After she pulled her hands approximately two feet apart, she dropped them in a vertical pattern. The wavering gold pattern followed and the tugging intensified. The heat felt good. Even though it was burning, it provided relief.

She began to hear inhuman screaming and shrieking. The shrieking sounded as if it were coming from inside the golden lines she was creating, while the screaming sounded as if it were coming from around her.

Suddenly, her hands were violently knocked apart. She screamed and fell forward as intense pain ripped through her body. Then Holden was in front of her and she registered the sounds of grunts and swords clashing.

# CHAPTER FIFTEEN

Holden had come awake to intense heat and shrieking sounds. As he opened his eyes, he saw Gabriella sitting up and a brilliant rainbow streaking from the center of her hands up into the sky. Then he saw four men running toward them, from both edges of the meadows. Two men wore green and two were clad in black. Something was screaming from behind where they had slept. He scrambled to toss his cloak away and grab his sword, while trying to discern where the screaming was coming from. It was confusing and chaotic. The sun was also high in the sky, so they had obviously both fallen asleep and slept well into the morning.

He unsheathed his sword, turned and looked toward the sound. In horror, he watched as their horses thrashed on the ground, bloody and screaming. They were still tied to the trees. It was almost unbearable to watch and he started shaking at the sight. He couldn't understand what was affecting the horses. It was horrific, as if their blood was being pulled from them. He turned around at the

111

sound of the men shouting at them. In the chaos, Holden couldn't make out what they were yelling.

One of the men in black stopped running and pulled a bow from where it was seated on his shoulders. Notching an arrow, he aimed at Gabriella.

In an instant, Holden was at the foot of the man with the bow. He slashed upwards with his sword, knocking the bow from the man's surprised hands. Holden stabbed the man in the thigh to disable him, then turned and ran back toward Gabriella. If this man had meant to shoot Gabby, he wasn't sure what the other men intended to do to her.

He arrived as a man in green and one in black each raised their swords and swiped down at Gabriella's arms. They knocked her to the ground and she screamed. The rainbow disappeared, but the gold still glimmered in the air. Holden felt like he was going to explode with fear for his sister. He stepped between her and the men, engaging them both with his sword. Within minutes, he had disarmed the two, and then the third one in green. He stabbed each in a thigh, like he had the first man with the bow.

He didn't want to hurt them, as they were leprechauns and he was sure that he shouldn't. Yet he wanted to protect his sister and himself. Breathing hard, he looked around. The men were on the ground, groaning and grabbing at their legs to stop the flow of blood . Holden stared at the horses, deadly still and bloody. Shaking his head, he stepped over to his bedroll, grabbed his sword belt, buckled it as fast as possible, grabbed his bow and quiver, looped them over his shoulders, picked up his cape and tossed it around his shoulder, clasping it at his sternum. Then he grabbed Gabriella's cloak, dropped it over her shoulders and fastened the clasp also. He ignored their backpacks and bedrolls.

He pulled her to her feet. She seemed dazed and in a lot of pain, yet was seeming to become coherent. She blinked her eyes and focused on him.

"What . . . what just happened, Holden?" she asked, glancing around. She winced as she moved her head. He could tell the pain radiated through her entire body, like each movement was excruciating. Her focus was only on him, which was good. He didn't point out the groaning, gasping men and or want her to see the lifeless horses.

"I don't know, but we should get out of here immediately. More might come." He grabbed her hand and tugged her forward. A shiver rippled through him. The feeling reminded him of what it felt like when they would grab Uncle Robert's hand and run at high speed. Holden didn't think any more about it. He tightened his hold on Gabriella's hand, made sure it was clenched firmly in his, and ran.

He led them through the trees and onto the dirt path they had come from the night before. They sped up the mountain, and he tried to navigate the twists and turns as they hurtled forward. He could feel Gabby tiring and tugging at his hand. Instead of slowing, he kept up the pace, scared to stop.

Ahead, a curve came up and the dirt road forked. Holden took the fork to the right, yet there was an unexpected sharp drop in the road. He released Gabriella's hand as they both plunged down a steep hill.

# CHAPTER SIXTEEN

Once he stopped tumbling, Holden lay stunned, on his back. Twisting his head, he spotted Gabriella next to him, on her side,. groaning, so he knew she was alive. He turned his head back and closed his eyes. He was breathing hard and shaking. For a few moments, he tried to slow his breathing and also come to terms with what just happened. Somehow, he had the strength and speed to reach not only the first bowman, but disable him and then return and fight off the other men. He wasn't sure what to think. Did that mean he was getting his abilities? Did a half human, half leprechaun get abilities?

Holden pushed himself to his feet, rolling his shoulders. As he did this, he realized that his bow and quiver were missing. Patting his waist, he found his sword intact and hanging against his thigh. With a quick glance around, he spied his bow lying not too far away. The quiver was a few feet from it, yet the arrows were scattered all down the steep hill they had just tumbled down. He quickly moved forward and retrieved his bow, quiver and the arrows. Once he slung the bow and quiver over his shoulder, he turned and walked back to where Gabriella was still lying on the ground. He crouched down and reached toward her.

"Get up, Gabby." Holden grabbed her arm and attempted to pull her into a sitting position. Gabby leaned forward for an awkward moment, then sprawled back onto the forest floor. She groaned and rolled from her back to her side.

"I can't," she said.

"You have to." Holden knelt down beside her. "You have to get up now. Now," he repeated as he pulled at her arm again.

"Holden, I . . . I can't. My whole body hurts." She kept her eyes closed as she spoke.

At the distant sound of horns blowing, Holden shook Gabby harder. He had to get his sister back on her feet and move from where they were. They were exposed at the bottom of the ridge they had tumbled down, near the trail. He had to help her walk, to find a better place to hide.

"Give me a minute. Let me just lay here for a second." She tried to swat him away. He brushed her hand aside and pulled her arm up again.

"Do you want a minute or a second? Because we don't have either," he said.

"I know, but it hurts," she whined.

"Let it hurt later and get up now. Now, Gabby." Holden stood and put his hands on his hips. He had to figure out something. They had to get off the road soon, or be discovered. "Stand up now or I'm going to kick you," he said as he looked down at her.

She opened her eyes and glared up at him. "You wouldn't dare, Holden," she growled.

"Yes, I would," he raised both eyebrows at her. He was serious. If she didn't move, then the next soldier or person to come down the road would discover them. He couldn't and wouldn't let that happen.

"Okay, okay! I'm getting up," she nearly screamed. Rolling over onto her stomach, she placed her palms down and slowly pushed herself to her knees. Holden reached down, slipped his hands under her arms and helped her to her feet.

Once she was on her feet, Holden put her arm around his shoulder and helped her limp away.

Holden tried to pull Gabriella along faster, but they weren't getting very far off the main path. They were exposed where they were and a good distance from the trees. There was no other shelter or place to hide.

"Holden, I'm trying to move faster," Gabriella wheezed as she stumbled along.

"I know, Gabby," Holden said. She was leaning on him quite a bit and getting heavier with each step. They had to make it to the trees. The distance was shortening, but perhaps not fast enough. They had to make it. That way, if anyone came down the path, they would have a chance to avoid discovery.

After a few more moments, Gabriella straightened and took her weight off Holden. Her breathing also evened out and sounded steadier, less ragged.

Holden jogged ahead a few steps and went into the tree line. The trunks were densely spaced, with about a horse's body length between each of them. He wanted to hike in further to hide. After glancing through the trees one more time, he twisted back and waved at Gabriella to follow.

Holden went past two more trees, taking them deeper into the forest, when a loud crash in front of him almost knocked him off his feet. He jumped back and grabbed the nearest tree, missed it and teetered for a moment until he regained his balance. Gabriella gasped from behind him. A black reptilian creature, with large black wings and covered in scales, landed right in front of him. It was the size of a Great Dane. It had snake-like skin, with perfectly proportioned scales, and lean, defined muscle mass. Chiseled shoulders and haunches slid down to razor sharp talons.

"What is that thing?" Gabriella pointed at it. The creature shook, then folded its wings, and sat on its back legs.

"It looks like a flipping dragon." Holden stepped forward. The dragon dropped to all fours and stepped toward Holden. It tilted its head to the side and stared at him.

"I thought there weren't any dragons here." Gabriella smacked his back, hard. Holden flung a hand behind him and smacked her in return. It wasn't his fault a dragon had just landed in front of them.

"Me too, but . . ." Holden shrugged. He didn't think any dragons were supposed to be here in the leprechaun realm, but he also didn't know very much about this place. The dragon stepped closer until it was almost touching him. Even though he ought to be scared, he wasn't. Meeting a dragon for the first time was fascinating. Layers of ebony scales rippled down the lean body. Holden glanced down and his eyes widened; the talons were sharp as a lion's and could shred him in seconds. He hoped the thing couldn't breathe fire, because if it could, they'd be toast before they could turn and run away.

"Aren't dragons supposed to be bigger than that?" Gabriella quizzed him.

"I don't know. This is the first dragon I've met," he said and tilted his head toward the glossy V-shaped black head that was now sniffing his shoulder. He twisted and looked directly at the creature.

"Well, hello."

Huge yellow eyes with obsidian-colored slits in the middle of each locked onto his. Holden tried not to blink but could not hold a stare as long as it could. The eyes reminded him of a gecko. Geckos were harmless, maybe this thing would be too. Holden blinked. The creature blinked back at him. It had no eyelashes. He couldn't remember if Geckos had eyelashes.

"Who are you, I wonder," he murmured to it as he reached a hand forward and touched the scaly face. The dragon lunged back and hissed, flapping its wings furiously. Leaves and dirt flew about, pelting them. For such a small dragon, it had enormously powerful wings.

"Holden!" Gabriella lifted her arms to shield her face from the flying debris. The dragon hopped back a step and beat its wings faster, yet it didn't lift off.

"Woah!" Holden shouted at it. He lifted his arms and held them aloft, attempting to calm it down. The dragon lifted its wings higher and beat them even faster.

Gabriella began retreating, backing up to the road. "Not working, not working," she grumbled.

"No kidding," Holden growled back and ducked his head to dodge a flying branch. It caught his cheek and gouged deep enough to cause him to wince. If he didn't stop the dragon, it would either hurt one of them or cause someone to notice them. If Uncle Robert were here, he'd know what to do, but his uncle had abandoned them in the bookstore. That made him hurt more than the gouge on his cheek. Holden gritted his teeth. He could do this, he certainly didn't need his uncle for this. He'd take care of the dragon and get them back on their journey.

Squeezing his eyes shut, he began to imagine the same dragon, but even bigger. He imagined it roaring and scaring this dragon. Immediately, a loud roar echoed through the forest. Holden's eyes flew open and there, standing next to him was a huge dragon, just as he had imagined. It was shimmering though and not quite fully formed. He could see through it to the forest beyond.

He was doing this. He was creating it. He could feel the power of the image rippling through his body. It felt like holding something incredibly heavy and having to concentrate really hard on not dropping the object. The weight of the unknown object, the concentration it required to create the image, pulled at his entire body, not just in one spot. He focused harder, more on the image in his mind of a fully formed dragon, and the flesh of the dragon solidified into dense, dark scales.

"Again," he moved his lips. The dragon he had created opened its mouth and another roar ripped through the area, as it raged at the smaller dragon in front of it. The little dragon folded its wings and dropped its head low, cowering before the bigger dragon. Holden kept the image of the big dragon in his mind and approached the little dragon.

"Now be still," he said as he leaned forward and set his hand on the dragon's head. When the dragon didn't move, he tried a single stroke. The little dragon looked directly at him, but kept its head low. Holden stroked again, and then again. It sniffled, as if it were offering an apology for causing a ruckus.

Branches snapped as Gabriella approached from behind. Her mouth hung wide open. The large dragon disappeared.

"Seriously, did you just do that?" she asked as she gaped at him.

"Yeah, I think so." Holden was even more tired now than before, but he kept stroking the dragon. They were down two horses, but up one dragon. He wasn't sure this one was large enough to carry his weight. He decided not to test it.

"Wow." Gabriella stepped up next to him.

"I know." He grinned at her, excited. He wasn't sure how he made it happen, other than getting upset and imagining a larger dragon. Maybe that was all there was to it, intense concentration and the wish to make something happen. He couldn't wait to try it again, but only after he had rested. Rest, however, wouldn't come for a long time. They had to get back on the road to the Dark Kingdom.

"Are we going to leave it here?" Gabriella reached out to touch the dragon's head. It let her. She began to stroke it, like it was their new pet dog. Although this pet was a lot more ferocious than a dog.

"I don't think we should keep it. I think dragons are wild animals." Holden stopped stroking the creature and let his hand fall to his side.

"Maybe, but he's awful cute, in a dark lizardy sort of way." Gabriella didn't stop petting the dragon. She stepped closer, and the dragon leaned into her, nuzzling the front of her skirt. It liked being petted. Holden shook his head and stepped back. What a strange little creature.

An honest to goodness real dragon. Even though he knew an entire world existed, one where his mom was from, he never imagined that he would ever be allowed to travel to it, let alone see a dragon.

"Gabby," he said, "we seem to be able to do a lot more, now that we're here. Does that worry you?"

Gabriella stilled her hand, and let it rest on the dragon's head. "It doesn't worry me. But it makes me wonder why mom never told us much, and never brought us here."

"Me too," Holden said.

"She had to have a good reason." Gabriella patted the dragon's head, and then removed her hand also. The dragon perked up and looked at them, entreating them to pet it more.

Holden smiled, and stepped forward to give it a last pat also. "Okay, little dragon, time for you to go." Holden waved his hand, shooing it away.

The dragon sat there, unmoving.

"Shoo!" Holden said.

The dragon didn't move.

"Go." Holden put both hands on its chest and pushed it. It still didn't move.

"Come on, go," he said louder and pushed harder. The dragon didn't budge. It leaned down and blew a stream of air into his hair, ruffling the dark strands.

"No." Holden reached up and tried to push the dragon's face away. It only blew harder.

To make matters worse, Gabriella began laughing.

"No. No. No! Go away!" Holden huffed and turned around to lean against the dragon, using all his weight to push against it. He kept pushing until he slid down the length of the dragon, exhausted. He lay sideways, half sprawled on the ground, and half resting against one of the dragon's sinewy legs. He tried to ignore the razor sharp claws that were gripping the dirt next to his hand. He was too tired.

"Great job telling it what to do." Gabriella snickered.

"You try," Holden scrunched his nose at his sister.

Another horn blew in the distance. Holden and Gabby looked at each other, startled. Someone was looking for them. From behind him, Holden felt the dragon stiffen. It was standing taut on all fours, and even though it had scales and no hair, it appeared that its scales were raised, wary. Holden scrambled up to a standing position.

"We need to get rid of the dragon," Gabriella told him.

"I know," Holden snapped at her. He'd been trying to do that.

"We can't hide with a dragon too." She flung her hands in the air.

They were both tired. An idea popped into Holden's head. He clapped his hands together. "Ha!" he shouted at the dragon and smacked it. The dragon jumped back surprised, all four feet off the ground, and landed about two feet away. It gave him a wounded look.

A rumbling sound filtered from the ridge above them. The dragon looked at Holden and Gabby, then to the ridge. It looked back at them for a moment, unfurled its wings and in one wide sweeping motion, lifted up from the ground. With a few more flaps of the large wingspan, at least four times of that of its body, it took off over the tree tops and disappeared.

# Chapter Seventeen

The rumbling turned into a more defined sound of horse's hooves beating a fast percussion on the ground. It now came from right over the ridge. Holden glanced behind them and saw a horse and rider cresting the ridge. He twisted his head, and gave Gabriella a hard look.

"Be ready," he said.

"Yeah, right. Cause this morning has been so much fun already." She scowled at him and kicked the dirt, but squared her shoulders, preparing to fight. They were both exhausted and dirty, and not looking forward to another skirmish of any sort.

The riders spotted them and moved in their direction. Within seconds, three boys mounted on horses surrounded them. Holden drew his sword and held it out in front of him, preparing to defend them both if needed.

"Hey, we saw the battle," a tall boy not much older than Holden said. He was dressed all in black, his cloak was black, the inside lined in crimson. Like the two men in the meadow, his clothing was that of the Dark Kingdom. A sword hung from his hip also. "We mean you no harm. We're actually here to help you."

"Yeah, we're here to help," an older boy spoke up. He appeared to be closer in age to Gabriella and was also dressed in the colors of the Dark Kingdom. "It won't be too long before more soldiers come."

Holden looked at them, not sure what to do. They were right though; more men and most likely soldiers would be coming after them, and soon. He had wounded four men; two horses were dead. Even if he couldn't explain the horses' deaths, he was responsible for hurting the men.

"How did you fight off four grown men?" The first boy asked.

"I, um . . ." Holden trailed off. He wasn't sure what to say. He didn't sense these boys were threatening, but their clothing identified them as from the Dark Kingdom, the place where his mom was being held.

A thump next to him distracted him. He turned around to see Gabriella slumped on the ground, out cold. He dropped to his knees and set his sword down.

"Gabriella. Gabby!" He shook her shoulders but she didn't wake up. Her head rolled on the ground, and her eyes stayed closed. He could see her chest rising and falling, so she was alive, just unconscious. Great. Just great, he thought. What a perfect time to pass out.

Holden looked up at the trio on horseback. After a moment, he realized that he had little choice but to trust them. Sighing, he stood, sheathed his sword, then knelt down and tugged Gabriella into a sitting position. He looped one of her arms around his neck. She kept her eyes closed and moaned in pain.

"Here, let me help." Another boy had dismounted and looped Gabriella's other arm over his shoulder also. He appeared to be between the ages of the other two boys. All three had dark brown hair, colored much like Holden and Gabriella. "Let's put her on my horse."

"Wait. No. We don't know you," Holden said. They had obviously witnessed the battle from some vantage point and were from the Dark Kingdom, but other than that, they were strangers. He wanted to draw his sword again; he was so confused.

"Oh yeah, of course not," the boy helping to carry Gabby said with a grin. "I'm Wyatt."

"I'm Cayden," the older boy said from where he was seated on his horse.

"I'm Hunter," the youngest said with a grin and a quick wave.

"Ah, I'm Holden," Holden introduced himself and looked at Gabby. She had her head down and was breathing hard again. "This is my sister, Gabby."

"Yeah, she doesn't look so good. During the scuffle you had, we saw the soldiers knock her down. That's when we started to ride down from where we were watching," Cayden said. He dismounted and walked over to them.

"We lost you for a while when you sped up and disappeared. You were a blur," Wyatt told Holden as he helped to hold up Gabby.

"Wyatt, let's put her up on my horse." Cayden pulled his horse around.

"She seemed to recover once we stopped." Holden told them. He wasn't sure what was happening with Gabriella, but he felt close to passing out himself. After battling the soldiers, running up the mountain at an increased speed, then projecting a dragon, he felt darn near spent. "And, I'm not sure we should go with you. Even though we just met, we still don't know you." Holden sighed.

"Don't worry. We're harmless, well kinda sorta harmless," The one introduced as Hunter chuckled. "We aren't supposed to be out and about, but no one pays any attention to us." Hunter looked at them, smiling wide. It was as if he thought the entire situation was quite amusing.

"Search parties from both kingdoms are going to be dispatched after you soon enough," Cayden said. "What you just did to those soldiers, fighting them off and then running away with your sister is going to draw attention. Do you really want to be found here? I realize you don't know us, but we are the only ones around offering help right now." Cayden looked directly at Holden.

"You make a good point," Holden said. He didn't want to be around. He wanted to be curled up somewhere, sleeping.

"Then come with us. We'll take you back to the castle and hide you there," Wyatt said, a big grin splitting his face. "We'll hide you until we figure out why soldiers from both kingdoms just rushed you."

"The castle? The Dark Castle?" Holden asked.

"Yep. That's where we live," Hunter said from his perch atop his horse.

"Our uncle is the Dark King." Wyatt frowned and shrugged. "I couldn't care less that he's my uncle." He then rolled his eyes for good measure.

"Uh oh. He is?" Holden said. That meant these were the Dark King's nephews. That probably was not good.

"Yep," Cayden confirmed.

"But don't worry," Wyatt told him. "The Dark King doesn't pay any attention to us. Our older brothers are more important."

"You have more brothers?" Holden asked, incredulous. He remembered that Leprechauns didn't have many children.

"Yep. My mom had five boys total," Cayden said. "We are the youngest."

"Wow." It was all Holden could think to say.

"Yeah, we get that quite often, " Wyatt said and gave another exaggerated eye roll. "Five boys is extremely unusual. We hear the whispers behind our backs."

"Come on, let's get her up and out of here. We can talk later." Cayden snapped them back to attention. He held the reins to still his horse as Wyatt and Holden handed Gabriella up to him. He settled her in front and Gabriella fell back against him, exhaustion sketched into her facial features.

"Hold her tight, don't let her fall," Holden said. He and Gabriella might have been arguing with each and smacking each other a few moments before, but she was his sister and he didn't want anything to happen to her.

"Don't worry. I've got her," Cayden assured him. He put his arms around Gabriella to hold her steady and settled the reins.

"Here, you can ride with me," Wyatt called down to Holden. He had already mounted his horse. Wyatt put his hand down to Holden, to help pull him up. Holden grabbed his outstretched hand, put one foot in the stirrup and swung himself up and onto the back of the horse.

"Are we ready?" Hunter asked as he turned his mount and headed to the path.

"Yep," Wyatt said and looked over to Cayden. Cayden nodded at him and they both started forward.

After a few trots, the horses broke into a gentle gallop and began to climb the ridge. Holden looked over at Cayden and Gabby, to ensure that Gabriella was secure. Cayden had a tight grip on her as they climbed up and over the ridge. Holden relaxed, knowing that Cayden had her and that she wouldn't fall.

Once they had crested the ridge and the path settled into a slope, weaving its way up the mountain again, the boys increased the speed of the horses. They were at a full gallop and thundering as the ground sped past.

"So, how did you do that, with the soldiers?" Wyatt shouted at Holden.

"Do what?" Holden shouted back.

"Fight off four grown soldiers?"

"I really don't know. It just happened. I saw a soldier raise a bow towards my sister and I just reacted. I was scared that he was going to shoot her."

"It's pretty flipping amazing. You were so fast. You must be getting your abilities now," Wyatt shouted again over the sound of the horses. "I wish I could."

"Yeah, I really don't understand," Holden was half human, so he shouldn't have been able to do it at all, and not at his age. From what he'd understood, Leprechauns started to get their abilities right before adulthood. That was still a few years away for him. The fact that he had fought and injured four grown leprechaun men, both Light and Dark soldiers, surprised and scared him a little. It made him wonder if he was half human at all. If he wasn't, then who was his dad? His mom had always been very careful to answer only certain questions. But now he needed to get some real answers and not the "one day I will tell you" promise again from her.

Did that mean Gabriella was getting her abilities too? She was at the right age to be getting them. Maybe it was that she was half human too, and being here in this realm was affecting them both in some strange manner. Holden felt more determined than ever to find his mom. He was sure that when Gabriella felt better, she'd be asking the same questions.

"Here." Hunter slowed, pulled his horse back and handed something toward Holden. It was a thick hunk of bread and cheese, both of which looked like they had been ripped from larger pieces. To Holden it didn't matter. He was starving, but had been too occupied and worried up until this point to even consider his hunger.

"Thanks," he said as he leaned over and took the food. Hunter smiled and kicked his horse forward. Holden shoved hunks of bread and cheese in his mouth as the group continued to ride. With each bite, he felt less tired and more nourished.

# CHAPTER EIGHTEEN

They rode at a breakneck pace along the mountain path for many hours. Only when the horses began to tire did they slow. It was easier to talk when they weren't thundering around sharp bends and over steep inclines. The entire time, even being jostled around, Gabriella had slept. Cayden kept a firm grip on her, and she never slipped, no matter how treacherous and difficult the terrain.

The farther north they traveled up the mountain, the colder it was becoming. Holden was glad they had the black, crimson lined cloaks Tay had given them before they stepped through the portal. His was heavy and kept him warm. Although at this point he wished he had the same color clothing as Wyatt, Cayden and Hunter. He didn't want to stand out when they arrived at the Dark Castle.

"How much farther until we get to the castle?" Holden asked Wyatt.

"About another two hours. We aren't supposed to be outside the castle grounds, but no one cares what we do.

We were heading down to the borderlands when we came across you and the soldiers. With the impending battle, we wanted to be as far away from the castle as possible for a few days."

"I'm glad you did." Holden wasn't sure what the next few hours would bring, especially when they arrived at the Dark Castle, but he instinctively trusted Wyatt and his brothers. He hoped his instincts weren't wrong.

"Yeah, me too." Wyatt tossed a grin back at Holden. "It's not just us in trouble this time."

Holden laughed. "Do you get in trouble often?"

"Too much." Cayden frowned and pulled alongside them. They had been forced to ride single file for so long, Holden didn't realize until now that the path had widened.

"Yeah, but I'd rather be in a little bit of trouble than living under our uncle's thumb," Wyatt told his brother.

Cayden smiled in response and nodded a few times. "That's very true."

"Wait, you said impending battle. What battle?" Holden asked Wyatt.

"Our uncle has opened a portal to the human world, and intends to open a larger one, to go find his son," Wyatt explained as he patted his horse, sweaty from exertion.

"Why? What happened to his son?"

"He's been missing for over fourteen years now. I found a clue a few weeks ago, when we were exploring and went to a place we weren't supposed to be. I came across a scroll. It was a note from our cousin, one that had been hidden in the wall and written before he disappeared. It explained to his father how he was in love and going to live in the human world."

"Are you serious?" Holden thought his mom was the only one who lived in the human world.

"Yep, kinda funny he took off for love, to go live with the humans. Our uncle can't stand humans, so cousin Jeremias must have fallen in love with a human." Wyatt laughed. Holden didn't laugh with him. His mom must have fallen in love with a human too. Why else would she have lived in the human world? He kept quiet.

"Yeah, it is pretty darn interesting. Fourteen years ago, scouts were sent to search for him in all the different realms. He was never located." Cayden shrugged. His movement disturbed Gabby, who woke up and stretched.

"Where in the world?" she said, looking around her and down at the horse she was on.

"Good morning, sleeping troll," Holden tossed at her.

"I'm not a troll, you maggot." Gabriella scowled back at him.

"Ha! I can feel the sibling love!" Wyatt laughed at them both.

"Yeah, it's love all right." Gabriella continued to scowl and take in her surroundings. "No, seriously, where are we? And who are you guys?" Gabriella looked back at the boy holding her. She didn't seem so sure of him, and stiffened.

"I'm Cayden." Cayden gave her a short quick nod.

"I'm Wyatt." Holden's riding partner grinned at her.

"I'm Hunter," the one riding ahead of them shouted back, a little louder than he needed too.

"Um, hi," Gabriella said. Holden could see she wasn't sure what else to say. He laughed. It was funny that she was at a loss for words, because she always had something to say about everything.

"What happened with the soldiers, Gabby, why'd they hit you?" Holden asked. He'd been wanting to ask her, but with everything happening so fast, this was his first opportunity. "And what was all that light?"

"Something strange, I don't know how to explain it," she replied.

"You were starting to open a portal," Cayden told her.

"But that's impossible." Gabriella half turned in her seat to give him a puzzled look.

"Why is it impossible? That's what you were doing. I could sense it, and so could the soldiers. It wasn't a portal to somewhere you should have been opening though," Cayden told her.

"But I can't open portals. I don't have any abilities," Gabriella argued.

"Well, you might not think so, but you were opening a portal. Of that I'm positive," Cayden said.

Gabriella looked at Holden. He shrugged. Was it true, was she getting leprechaun abilities now too?

"Gabby, I think something is affecting us, being here," Holden said. She frowned and kept looking at her hand.

"I think so too. Something's happening to me," she said slowly.

"We're heading to the Dark Castle," Holden told her, as if sensing her hesitation and curiosity. He also wanted to switch their conversation before the boys started asking questions. He shouldn't have said anything, but it came out anyway.

"We are?" Gabriella was surprised. First, she'd been told that she'd been opening a portal and now she was told they were heading to where their mom was being held captive.

"Yep, should be there in about two hours," Wyatt answered.

"We have to pick up the pace if we want to make it there in two hours," Cayden said and kicked his horse forward. Wyatt and Hunter did the same. The road was still an incline, but not as steep and with fewer curves than before.

# CHAPTER NINETEEN

Tired, they slowed the sweating horses to a walk after nearly two hours of hard, relentless riding. The road had become narrow and rocky. Snow lined either side of it and large, sharp boulders protruded everywhere. It was apparent they had reached the tree line, as trees had become spars. The sky darkened with gray clouds.

Gabriella had been thinking of the morning's events. Her hands had been burning hot and she'd felt like someone was calling to her from a dream. It was as if someone were shouting her name, urging her on. In her dream, she had put her hands together, because the burning had been so bad. Light had spilled from them. It was an incredible sight and mesmerized her. She started to spread her hands, to make the light bigger and that was when the soldiers had knocked her hands apart. The light had disappeared and pain instantly gripped her entire body. She screamed, then Holden was there next to her, drawing his sword and striking the swords of the soldiers who had struck her. After the threat was gone, Holden had grabbed her. They raced down the path, farther away from the borderlands until they stumbled down the hill and met the dragon. The events after that were incredibly fuzzy but one thing she felt certain of was that she had not been opening a portal. Yet, running with Holden had been like running with Uncle Robert. Holden had somehow increased their speed.

Gabriella's stomach growled. She felt insanely hungry. "Do you have anything to eat?" she turned to ask Cayden.

"Oh, I'm sorry. I should have known you'd be really hungry after expending the energy to open that portal," he apologized. "Hunter," he yelled ahead, "would you hand us something to eat?"

Hunter pulled his horse to a halt. He reached into a pouch that was latched onto his saddle and pulled out a hunk of bread and an apple, then leaned over to hand them to Gabriella.

"Thanks," Gabriella said, biting into the apple with a crunch.

"Of course. Sorry I didn't think of it earlier," Hunter apologized with a sheepish grin.

"No worries," she said. Each bite made her feel less tired and more energized. Within moments, she had devoured the bread and apple. She even ate the apple core, something she would never before have considered. Today, it was sustenance and it was gone before she could fully consider not eating it. She eyed Hunter's pouch, wondering if there was more food inside.

A loud, unsettling screech erupted behind them. Cayden's horse tensed but did not dance, shy away or even attempt to bolt. Holden tightened his grip on Wyatt and swung his head around to look.

The food pouch forgotten, Gabriella turned to look also. What greeted her gaze was the dragon from earlier, flying up the mountain trail toward them.

Although small, in flight the glistening ebony body was ferocious looking as it clawed its way toward them. It was flapping its large wings, and Gabriella could see that they were iridescent and slightly see-through. She'd missed that when they were on the ground. Yet at the time, she'd been trying to shield her face, and not paying full attention to its wings.

Once it got close to them, it changed the beat of its wings, and stayed in a holding pattern about ten feet off the ground and about fifty yards away. It opened up its beak and let out another shrill, bone-jarring shriek.

Holden shot Gabriella a sheepish, awkward look while Wyatt and Cayden exchanged horrified looks. Hunter edged his horse closer to their group, falling back from the lead he had taken earlier.

"How did a dragon get loose in our realm?" Hunter shook his head slowly. His glaze was glued to the creature and his body tense. His hand moved slowly toward his sword.

Holden twisted his face at his sister. While everyone else's gaze was locked on the dragon, Holden and Gabriella were exchanging guilty expressions.

"I think it's my fault," she admitted.

Wyatt twisted around in his saddle and said, "What?"

"If it was a portal I opened, I think it was a portal to where this came from." The shrieks and roars of the dragon had matched the sounds she remembered from her dream, or what she had thought was a dream.

"Oh, that might be about as bad as the battle that's going to happen soon," Hunter spoke up. He'd been a silent observer for most of their conversations, but the appearance of the dragon roused him enough to speak this time.

"Here, let me down." Holden slid off the horse he was sharing with Wyatt. He walked a few feet toward the dragon and stood waiting as the dragon dove toward him and landed. All eyes were glued on both him and the dragon.

"Holden, that's not a good idea," Cayden called. "Dragons are dangerous and vicious animals, no matter their size." Cayden nodded to his brothers and the three of them slowly began to draw their swords.

Gabriella reached back and put her hand on Cayden's sword hand, stopping him from fulling pulling it out of his scabbard.

"Actually," she said, "We've already met this thing."

"What?" three voices said in startled unison.

Gabby shrugged. "A bit after the soldiers attacked us in the field, once we came to a stop, it landed in front of us. We weren't sure what it was. We guessed a dragon."

"Yeah, it's a dragon alright. A young one." Wyatt eyed Holden, his hand still on his half-drawn sword.

Holden stopped within a foot of the dragon and extended a hand. The dragon stepped forward and put his head under Holden's hand. Holden petted it and the dragon stepped closer. Holden laughed. It only wanted affection.

"What in the realm of all that is unknown . . ." Cayden breathed and shifted his weight in the saddle.

"It appears to be a nice dragon," Gabriella felt compelled to explain. All three boys wore dumbfounded expressions and she guessed that this wasn't their usual dragon interaction.

"There are no nice dragons," Cayden disagreed.

"Nope, none," Hunter echoed.

"Well, maybe one," Wyatt countered and sheathed his sword fully, then pointed to Holden and the near-purring dragon. The dragon was twisting and turning his head beneath Holden's ministrations, attempting to get different parts stroked.

"The problem though, is how did it get here?" Cayden turned to ask Wyatt and Hunter. "Do you think it came through the portal? If so, we need to get back to the castle fast, and alert others. The portal cannot remain open, if it still is. More of these could slip through."

"Well, at least she only opened a small portal to the dragon world." Hunter lifted an eyebrow at Gabriella.

"I didn't mean to!" Gabriella twisted her face back at him.

"But you did it anyway," Wyatt shot back and edged his horse closer, "and now there's a dragon loose in the realm."

"It's not really loose in the realm. It did find us again." Gabriella scrunched her nose and lifted her chin at him.

"Stop, this isn't helping," Cayden said. "We need to find a solution before the dragon causes any issues. He pushed himself out of the saddle and slipped to the ground. With slow, measured steps he carefully approached Holden and the dragon.

Gabriella settled back, glad not to be perched halfway on the pommel any longer. She narrowed her eyes and shot Hunter another glance. He narrowed his eyes back at her.

"Think we should see if it will follow us?" Holden asked once Cayden stood next to him. The dragon had half an eye open and was looking up at the newcomer. It was almost purring, and content to have its head rubbed and petted like a cat.

"Well, I'm not sure what else to do with it." Cayden sighed and put his hands on his hips.

"I think that's a great idea," Gabriella called down from her perch.

"Bad, bad, bad idea," Hunter muttered from his.

"Brilliant idea!" Wyatt joined in the conversation with a big grin.

Holden stopped petting the dragon and turned around. He put his hand up. The dragon stood for a moment, cocked its head, then stepped over to Holden and rubbed its head under Holden's hand. After a few pats, Holden stepped back a few more steps, put up his hand and motioned for the dragon to come to him. It did.

Wyatt, Hunter and Gabriella all remained silent at this. Holden was getting a dragon to follow him! Cayden shook his head and folded his arms across his chest.

"Let's try from horseback now," Cayden called to Holden. He walked over to his horse and motioned for Gabriella to move forward again. She sighed and scooted forward.

Holden jogged over and Wyatt stuck a hand down, helping pull him up. The dragon remained where it was, looking at them.

After Holden reached down toward it, the dragon walked over to them. Holden leaned down and gave it a quick pat on the head, then straightened back up. "Okay, let's go and see what happens."

They urged their horses forward, and moved into single file on the mountain trail. Cayden and Gabriella took the lead, with Hunter in the middle and Holden and Wyatt bringing up the rear. Even though they were moving forward, their heads were all turned toward the dragon, watching it as they walked away.

After a few seconds, it opened its beak, gave a small shriek, tucked its wings closer to its body and started walking after them. For a creature that had such large wings and was known for flight, it walked along fine, shimmying back and forth slightly and making clicking sounds where its sharp claws hit rocks.

Cayden nudged his horse and picked up the pace more. Each of the riders did the same. The dragon increased its speed to match theirs.

# CHAPTER TWENTY

"What kingdom are you guys from?" Wyatt asked Holden.

"You wouldn't believe me if I told you," Holden said.

"Let me guess," Wyatt responded. "You're dressed in green, with a dark cloak, so you must be from the Ash and trying to blend into both the Light and Dark Kingdoms," Wyatt chuckled as if he had told a brilliant joke. Hunter laughed also.

"Not really." Holden smiled, glad that they had a sense of humor. Had they come across another party of leprechauns, there might have been a different outcome.

"Why are you dressed in both colors?" Cayden asked, flicking a quick glance to the dragon trotting along after them. "I understand that those who live in the borderlands mix colors, but usually only there. When people leave, they have one allegiant color."

Gabriella pulled her cloak tighter about her. She didn't really care that she had on mixed colors. She was glad for the warm cloak. She'd wear every color in the rainbow if it kept her warm. The higher they rode up the mountain, the colder it was becoming.

"You guys are from the Dark Kingdom. We're not," Gabriella said. She wasn't sure how much to tell them. They were helpful now and seemed nice, but she didn't know how things worked here. She was afraid that if she told them the truth, they would turn them in to someone in the Dark Kingdom. Well, everyone seemed nice except Hunter. She glared at his back.

"If you guys wanted to be away from the battle that's going to be happening, why are you headed back?" Holden asked, deflecting the question of where they were from for now.

"It seemed better to head back now," Cayden said, "after what we witnessed. We decided we'd try to find you guys, and if we didn't just head back. The Dark Castle has great places to hide. Even though the Dark King has opened a portal to the human world, and is intending to march on it, the Dark Castle is our home. We just didn't want to be there when the Light and Ash armies showed up. Now, it might not be a bad idea. There will be so much happening I don't think anyone will be looking for you there. Although, I'm not sure what we are going to do with the dragon."

"Why would the Light and Ash armies show up?" Gabriella asked. She knew the Light army was preparing for something. She wanted to know more details and if these boys had them, all the better.

"You really don't know?" Cayden asked.

"No," Gabriella said. Holden shook his head in agreement.

"Where are you guys from?" Cayden asked again, repeating Wyatt's earlier question.

Gabriella sighed. Perhaps it wouldn't hurt to trust them more. They'd already trusted them to this point. Worst case scenario, if the boys turned them in once they arrived at the Dark Kingdom, then hopefully they would be locked up with their mom. If that was the most awful thing that happened, it might not be so bad. She was still hoping their uncle would come after them, but that hope was dying with each hour they had been gone from the Light Castle.

"Well, we are . . . from the human world," she said.

In shock, Cayden pulled on the reins and stopped his horse, as did Wyatt and Hunter.

"No way!" Hunter exclaimed. He looked at Cayden and Wyatt. They all had equally puzzled looks on their faces.

"It's true. We are," Holden confirmed what his sister had told them. "We grew up in the human realm."

"Seriously?" Cayden questioned before he loosened the reins and urged his horse forward again.

"Yep," Gabriella told him. "We only came to this realm yesterday."

"Why did you grow up in the human realm?" Wyatt asked.

"We don't know. Our mom lives there, with us. Well, that is, she did," Holden said. "She disappeared about a week ago, and we came to find her."

"We're pretty sure she's being held at the Dark Castle." Telling this information to the three princes from the Dark Castle was risky. Yet as before, Gabriella decided once again to fully trust the boys. She didn't know why, but she felt right about doing so.

"Wow!" Hunter exclaimed. "No way."

"Your mom is the Light Princess?" Wyatt asked Holden.

"I guess," Holden shrugged.

They boys all stopped their horses again. Gabriella noticed that the dragon stopped too. It seemed to have picked up their rhythm and was moving when they moved. It hadn't taken off or flown away. At least not yet.

"We really need to think about this," Cayden told them all. "Our uncle is holding your mom prisoner. We're heading straight to the castle. We have a dragon with us. Do you really want to go there?"

"Our mom is there. We came for her." Gabriella twisted around to look at him.

"We can take you, but we can't help your mom escape. We can't." Hunter shook his head.

"I understand that, but we need to see our mom. Do you know if she's okay?" Holden asked.

"Yeah, from what we've heard, she's fine," Cayden said. "She arrived a week ago, opened a portal up right into the castle and demanded my uncle stand down from sending scouts and large search parties into the human world. They got in a heated argument and she ended up in a comfortable cell in the lower levels. After that, my uncle began to summon his army, to prepare to invade the human realm. He's going against the Council of Kings and breaking the treaty with the humans. That's why we wanted to be away from the castle for a few days."

"It was really weird that your mom marched right into the castle and started to make demands of my uncle," Wyatt agreed with his brother Cayden.

"Why was it weird?" Holden asked.

"Well, it was odd for a Light Leprechaun to show up like that, opening a portal right into the castle, but even stranger that it was the Light Princess that has been gone from the Light Kingdom for so long. All of our people have been whispering about it. Now you guys are here. This is so awesome." Wyatt grinned.

"It's not awesome," Gabriella snapped at him. "We just want to get our mom and go home."

"Go back to the human realm?" Cayden asked with a frown. "Why would you want to do that? You're leprechauns."

"We're half leprechaun," Holden told him.

"That's impossible," Cayden said. "If you were only half, you'd have no abilities. And we all know that you have abilities. We saw them. Not only do you have incredibly strong abilities, but you're getting them younger than you should. That means you are high royals, higher than we are. You're full leprechaun, all right."

"Cayden's right. You're definitely not half leprechaun," Hunter agreed.

Holden and Gabriella looked at each other, perplexed. The past two days had been a flurry of activity and confusion. So much had changed and there was so much that they didn't know. Too many unanswered questions, too many things happening so fast.

"Who's your dad?" Hunter asked.

Both Gabriella and Holden remained silent.

"You don't want to tell us?" Cayden asked.

"It's not that we don't want to tell you. We don't know," Gabriella said, sad at the thought of her father. She had always thought their dad was a human and had died in the fire when her mom had been pregnant with Holden. Gabby had to be half human. The side of her face was scarred because of the fire. If she were a leprechaun, the scars would have healed. She reached up to touch the patchwork of old scars on the left side of her face. Lifting her hair away from her face, she ran her fingers down the skin of her neck and by her ear. She felt along her scars and the partially deformed lobe of her ear.

"That's incredible," Cayden said, "and odd too. Leprechauns heal well. We don't get scars."

"I know. It's one of the reasons we always thought we were half human." Gabriella turned to look at him. "I don't understand why and how I have them, if I'm full leprechaun."

"I don't know either," Cayden said with an apologetic shrug. "Yet any human blood would dilute your bloodline enough that you would be weaker than the weakest of leprechauns. There'd be no way you could open a portal, not even with assistance. It's one of the reasons humans and leprechauns don't mix."

"Your dad has to be a royal. There's no other explanation," Wyatt mused.

"Why is there no other explanation?" Holden asked.

"Because of how powerful you are at such a young age," Cayden said. "He has to be a royal. Your mom is a royal, so that would explain it. Royal families are the most powerful leprechauns."

"What if it is Jeremias?" Hunter said, almost in awe.

"Who's Jeremias?" Gabriella and Holden asked in unison.

"Jeramias is our cousin, the Dark King's son. He is, well, was, the heir to the throne. But then he disappeared," Wyatt said.

"That would explain why the Dark King is invading the human realm," Hunter said, excited and bouncing on his horse. "If he somehow found out about you, that would give him the perfect reason to invade."

"Hunter, you just might be right," Cayden said.

The conversation was quickly forgotten as a low rumbling shook the mountain around them. Flashes of light and two rainbows shot up into the sky ahead of them, from above the ridge .

"Oh no," Wyatt said, looking up ahead.

"Uh oh," Cayden echoed.

"What?" Holden asked.

"What's happening?" Gabriella asked. She sensed that portals of some type had been opened. She could feel it, welling up from deep within her. The feeling was similar to the feeling in the bookshop and to what she had done, lower on the mountain.

"I think the Light and Ash armies are arriving," Cayden said. "This isn't good. We won't be able to enter the castle and hide you now. I had really hoped to make it back before this happened."

"I don't get it. If the Dark King opened the portal, why wait until two other armies showed up to invade?" Holden said.

"He's waiting to challenge the treaty. I'm pretty sure of it. It's what I would do," Cayden said. "If he doesn't challenge the kings, break the treaty with them first, then he pulls the entire realm into war with the humans, and also into war with each other."

"Yeah, I'd break the treaty with the other kingdoms first too," Hunter agreed. Wyatt nodded as well.

"Why not just invade the human world?" Gabriella was puzzled. Not that she wanted the Dark King to invade the human realm. It was odd thinking of home as the human realm now.

"If he breaks the treaty with the humans without first breaking it with the other kings," Wyatt said, "then it is an open declaration of war upon the other realms. He is smarter than that. He probably opened the huge portal to the human world to get the armies and other High Kings to come here, to outright do battle with them and then invade the human realm. At least, that is my guess. It's not like our uncle told us anything though."

Muffled shouts and and the sound of metal scraping against metal came from higher up. The children looked at each other. It was obvious some type of battle was about to happen ahead of them.

"Should we go?" Hunter asked. "I say we go see what is happening. Good or bad, I want to know." He was vibrating with a mix of barely suppressed excitement and worry.

"Let's find out," Holden agreed. It didn't take any more talking. All three boys spurred their horses on and rode up the last ridge to the Dark Castle grounds. The dragon followed.

As they crested the last hill and saw the full panorama exposed before them, Gabriella gasped. Cayden pulled his horse to a halt and the other two boys followed his lead.

A large black castle lay to the left, similar in size and dimension to the Light Castle, yet built with black stone. But that wasn't what caught Gabriella's attention. It was the hundreds, possibly a thousand or more men spread out next to the castle walls and pouring onto the mountain from two massive portals flanking the castle, each large enough to fit a two-story house through. A third portal stood open at the front of the castle.

From the leftmost portal came huge floating wooden ships. As soon as the ships came through, they tilted up and went higher in the sky, circling and hovering over the battle area. Archers lined the edges of the ships, with their bows at the ready, but not yet firing. There were four ships and they were starting to surround the castle. They looked like a mixture of an old Viking longboat and an old wooden battleship that might have been used by the English to fight the Spanish Armada during the reign of Queen Elizabeth.

"Woah," Holden whispered in awe, "floating ships."

"Yeah, that's the Ash army," Cayden said.

The Light army, dressed all in green and brown, poured out of the third portal to engage the Dark army that was amassing. Swords were being drawn.

"Holden, it's Mom!" Gabriella shouted and pointed down to the center of the castle grounds.

Their mom was kneeling next to two men arguing, hands at their swords. One of them was their grandfather, the Light King. Another was a man dressed in black and red.

As the two men shouted, Gabriella noticed her mom's arms were tied to a wooden slat above her head, keeping her hands apart. She was struggling with the bonds, trying to free herself while Light and Dark soldiers streamed around her and the two arguing men. Their mom was down there, in trouble, and in the midst of an impending battle.

Holden launched himself off the horse, and started to run toward the gathering. He slipped on the uneven ground, but righted himself before he pitched forward.

"Holden! No! You can't go down there in the middle of that," Wyatt hollered and jumped off his horse to grab him.

The dragon shook its head once, then pushed straight up, opened its wings and flew after Holden and Wyatt.

"Holden, no!" Gabriella shouted and tried to push off the horse she was on also. Cayden wouldn't let her. He held her firm.

"No, Gabriella. You cannot follow him. It's too dangerous," Cayden told her as she struggled against him. She tried to push his hands away, but he held tight.

"Let me go! Let me go now!" she screamed at him, trying to get down.

"Cayden, look," Hunter shouted, "the other part of the army is preparing to invade."

The sound of growing armies intensified.

Gabriella stopped struggling and looked to where Hunter was pointing. About fifty men from the Dark army were moving toward another large portal. Somehow Gabriella knew it was a portal to Earth. The large airships started moving towards this part of the army and the portal. The archers were trained on the section of the Dark army.

"Oh no," Hunter said, "if they start going through the portal, the Ash army will fire on them for sure." He grimaced, taking in the scene unfolding below them.

Gabriella searched for Holden. The men were all moving so fast, and blurring, making it difficult for her to see him. She finally spotted Wyatt running down the hill, chasing after Holden.

"Can't they close the portal and stop all this?" Gabriella asked, looking all over.

"I don't know," Hunter replied. "The portals are so large, it would take a few leprechauns. I've never seen anything like this before."

"They can't close the portal," Cayden said. "It's too large and the women won't be in the battle."

"Why won't the women be in the battle? Girls can fight too!" Gabriella scolded him, pushing to get down. "Let me down! I need to get down there to my mom and Holden!" she shouted at him again.

"No, you won't be able to defend yourself down there. Your mom is next to the Light and Dark Kings, and the Dark leprechauns would never hurt your mom." Cayden pointed down to where her mom was still struggling with her bonds.

"Are you sure?"

"Women leprechauns, especially the more powerful royal ones, open and close portals. They are too valuable.

It is absolutely forbidden to harm a royal female," Cayden explained.

"I still need to get down there," Gabriella begged, quieter this time. She knew this was about the portal to Earth. If she could close it, then there would be no need for a battle. The army couldn't invade if they couldn't get through the portal. "I need to get to the portal."

"We're not taking you to the portal. What would you do there? Run to Earth? It's too dangerous." Cayden almost sneered at her.

"I'm going to close the portal and end this." Gabriella turned and glared at him.

"You can't close it! It's too big for one person to close," Cayden told her, more forcefully.

"I have to try. I have this overwhelming feeling that I can do it. I don't know how, I just do. Please take me down there." Gabriella was almost panicking now. She'd lost track of Holden and her mom was still tied up and struggling.

The leprechaun armies were moving even faster toward each other across the expansive valley floor. It was evident the battle was impending. The air was like a moving sea, with ships hovering above, maneuvering about. At least they hadn't fired any arrows yet.

The Dark army was getting closer to the portal and the airships were closing in on them. Soon, it would be too late to stop them. If Wyatt was right, the Ash archers would soon begin firing on the Dark invading army. As of now, it was several armies running toward each other. Once the armies met and the archers started firing, the tide would turn bloody.

Hunter turned to Cayden and asked, "What if she's strong enough to close the portal on her own?"

"That's impossible, Hunter. There is no way," Cayden responded, holding Gabriella tight.

"But what if she could?" Hunter pressed. "If she's the daughter of two royal houses, she might be able to do it."

"Then the battle might be averted," Cayden breathed out slowly, wondering also.

"I say we let her try." Hunter nodded toward Gabriella.

"Do you have any metals?" Cayden asked her.

"What? No," she said, "We had some, but we left them behind."

"Yeah, and if you did have some earlier, they would have been the first thing used to create the portal you opened earlier today." Cayden shook his head at her.

"If I opened a portal," Gabriella said.

"You did. We saw it," Cayden confirmed.

"You're going to have to draw from the horses again," Hunter grimaced and patted his horse.

"Draw from the horses?" Gabriella asked, confused.

"Hunter, no," Cayden shook his head at Hunter, stopping him from explaining further. "Just do what you did earlier today. Concentrate on that," Cayden said, looking at her. His face was taut and his eyes bored into hers.

He turned toward his brother. "We need to go now, or it will be too late to stop this. Stay on my flank and go directly around the outside of the armies, straight to the Earth portal."

They clambered back up on their horses and headed down toward the valley. That's when the first swords clashed.

# CHAPTER TWENTY-ONE

Holden felt the burst of speed and energy boil up through him. He heard Wyatt shouting for him to stop but couldn't. They hadn't come this far to let anything happen to their mom. He put his head down and ran faster down the hill, dodging larger outcroppings and small rocks.

The blur of the armies approaching each other at an increased speed came into focus. When he'd been at the top of the hill, on horseback, it had been hard to make out, as they were moving so fast. Now that he was closer and moving at a similar speed, it was a sharper image. Then he saw it happen.

The Dark and Light armies met each other with swords raised and the first strike of the battle occurred. Leprechauns were clashing swords and disarming each other, then moving to hand-to-hand combat. He didn't see a single stab or bloody wound. It might be they fought a civilized type of combat before moving to a bloodier one. He felt a sharp tug on the back of his tunic and came to a stop at the bottom of the hill, where it flattened out. He turned to look behind, to see what had caught him.

Wyatt was running, still near the top, shouting for him to stop. It wasn't him. It was the small black dragon tugging on his shirt.

"Not you too." He turned to fully face the dragon.

"I need to go. You stay here!" he firmly pushed at the dragon's head. The dragon shook him off and head butted him in the mid-section. It sensed the danger of the quickly expanding battle that was approaching them. Within seconds, they'd be surrounded by it.

He pushed the dragon harder. "Stay here," he ordered. "Stay."

The dragon shook his head again, but didn't advance or push at him again. Holden and turned around and ran into the fray.

Two soldiers turned at him; he lifted his sword and caught the blows they delivered. He leaned back, then pushed forward. The solider on his right, a Dark Leprechaun, stumbled backward. This gave him the opportunity to put his full weight against the sword of the Light Leprechaun on his left. He swung downwards, then back up and the Light Leprechaun's sword clattered to the ground. He didn't have any time to pause, because the Dark Leprechaun's sword met his again. With a renewed vigor, he turned and disarmed him with two blows.

Over and over, he met sword for sword against many more leprechauns, both Dark and Light. Some pulled back when they saw how young he was, yet he continued to push through the throng of men toward his mother. He was faster and stronger than they were.

Whispers of the men he'd defeated began to follow him, but he ignored them. He had to get to the front. He didn't have time to stop; he was afraid that if he did, he might never reach his mother. Holden's muscles were burning and he was tiring. It was worse than the feeling he'd had after fighting the four soldiers to defend his sister, then racing to get away.

He shook his head and lifted his sword to strike at the next soldier. The soldier met his blow and pushed back. Holden stumbled and nearly lost his footing. The soldier swung his sword around and with a soft murmur of steel meeting steel, Holden's sword flew out of his hand. Holden's eyes widened.

"Stop, boy," the soldier ordered. He was a Dark Leprechaun.

"No," Holden glared up at him. "No!"

"This is a battle for men, not boys, you'll be harmed," another solider, one he had disarmed before, said from behind.

"I need to get to the front," Holden told them, breathing hard, exhausted.

The soldiers, one Dark, one Light, looked at each other, confused. They were here to support each of their kings, and a boy in the mix wasn't part of the plan. Not only was he a boy, but a boy with extraordinary strength and speed for his age.

Shouts from behind them all had them turning. A small dragon was flying overhead, stopping the men that hadn't been disarmed or hurt. It was his dragon. It hadn't stayed put as ordered.

The dragon gave Holden an idea. He wasn't sure if it would work, or if he could even pull it off with how exhausted he felt, but he had to try. He whistled, loud and sharp, up at the dragon.

The dragon heard his call and darted toward him. It flew straight down, lifting its wings to slow its descent. With a thump and growl at the leprechauns around Holden, the dragon landed in front of him. The dragon opened its mouth and hissed, causing a few of the men to step back.

Holden stepped forward and patted the dragon on the head. Gasps from both Light and Dark Leprechauns echoed from all around. He might not have stopped the battle, but around him, no one was fighting. They were too intent on the dragon and boy.

"Okay, here goes." He stopped patting the dragon's head. With a quick twisting pivot, he turned around to face the front of the battle and shut his eyes, picturing the largest, fiercest dragon possible. In his imagination, it was a monstrously huge, angry version of the small one standing next to him. He kept the image in his mind and willed it to take shape. A sensation of sickness gripped his stomach, yet he ignored it and willed the dragon to be even larger.

A deafening roar split the sky above him. Holden opened his eyes, looked up and there was his imagined dragon, flying directly overheard and toward the battle. The leprechauns from across the valley stopped mid-battle and looked up. Soon both armies were aware of the rapidly approaching beast. They shouted in unison, "Dragon!"

Holden smiled, happy they weren't seeing through the illusion. He imagined another roar. A huge bellow sounded above him. Not waiting for the reactions of more leprechauns, he ran right into the middle of the dumbfounded armies before him. He dodged between the leprechauns still fighting. His little dragon followed, close behind, darting as he did and mimicking his movements.

As he ran through the battle, the summoned dragon soared above them. Men shifted their focus from fighting each other to the large creature over their heads. Shocked gasps and shouts came from all around, as the fighting armies were falling into chaos. He thought it best to have the dragon fly a little higher, to keep the image as sharp as possible. These were grown leprechauns and some might see through the imagery and realize it wasn't a real dragon, but a ploy to distract them. If that happened, the battle would re-intensify and his progress would be impeded. So far, the armies were not paying attention to the boy and the dragon twisting and running between them, making their way to the head of the battle.

# CHAPTER TWENTY-TWO

The Ash army held steady, observing the battle below them but not becoming involved. They watched the boy and dragon wind their way through the armies below to the Dark Castle.

The Ash King held up a hand to his generals to halt his army from any further action. All the archers eased the pressure on their bows, keeping their arrows notched and standing ready, their eyes on the battle.

The Ash King looked at the large dragon. He could see through it to the armies fighting below. An incredibly strong leprechaun had created the image to fool the armies. He looked around to find the leprechaun that was controlling the image. All were engaged, except the boy who had arrived at the head of the battle. This boy was too young to create an image, let alone one so powerful. The king watched the boy slip between the two sparring kings below and cut loose the Light Princess. She turned and hugged the child.

He motioned to his generals again, and his archers lowered their bows. This unusual boy had just changed the course of the battle.

# CHAPTER TWENTY-THREE

The ride down on the outskirts of the battle felt like a lifetime to Gabriella, but it wasn't really that long. It was only minutes before they pulled abreast of the section of the Dark army preparing to invade the human world. Cayden rode right at the army and once they were mere feet away, he tugged sharply at the reins and pulled his horse to a halt. He jumped down and pulled Gabriella down after him.

"Hurry, do it now," he told her and pushed her at the portal. Gabriella stumbled for a moment, trying to stand up. They'd been riding for so many hours she'd become stiff. She didn't understand how Holden and Wyatt had jumped off their horses and run down the hill toward the battle.

She stumbled once more, then righted herself and hurried over to the portal. Soldiers in black and red lifted their swords, blocking her. Hunter rode up next to her and Cayden, and jumped off his horse.

"Halt! Halt!" Hunter cried at the Dark army. Many of the soldiers gave him a confused look. They knew he was the young Dark Prince, yet not the one giving the orders. One soldier mounted on a black stallion toward the back rode over to confront him.

"Hunter!" he said, his tone terse, "What are you doing?" He was an older teenager, and looked very much like Wyatt, Cayden and Hunter. His face was twisted into an angry scowl at the interruption.

"Ian, this is Jeremias's daughter. Halt the army now," Hunter shouted up at his brother. At the name Jeremias, shock filtered across Ian's face as well as many of the soldiers. Gabriella was surprised he said it. She looked at Cayden. He nodded in agreement with his brother. Even thought it was just a guess, it was the only playing card they had at the moment. If he was wrong, they'd all have some serious consequences to deal with later.

Cayden pushed at Gabriella's back, urging her forward. At the guards' confusion, Gabriella rushed forward and stepped around them, toward the portal. Cayden stayed behind her. Gabriella slowed, wavering for a moment. She was afraid she wouldn't be able to do anything, that her ability to close the portal would only be a hope and not a possibility, but she had to try. She came to a stop at the golden edge, stepped forward and put her hands up, willing them to get hot. Nothing happened. She closed her eyes and reached toward the set gold at the edge of the portal. It was cold and smooth to the touch, not at all hot like the one this morning.

She closed her eyes tighter and let her breath out and thought about her mom. She was down there tied up, and Holden was somewhere in the middle of the battle. She put her hands together on the portal. This time, her hands began to burn and warmth seeped out of them, touching the portal and warming it up. The pull began at her stomach and her hands heated even more. The pull was stronger than this morning, and much worse. She wanted to double over at the clenching, but she continued. After a few moments, she began to hear the inhuman screams again, much like this morning. She wavered for a moment, wanting to stop and see where the screaming and shouting was coming from. She let her hands slip down a bit and the clenching started to ease.

"No, Gabby, keep going," Cayden urged from behind her. "Ignore anything else."

She shook her head once and continued to press on the portal gold. It was softer, warming now. The awful clenching and pulling in her stomach returned. She bit her lip against the feeling, and pressed her hands together harder against the portal, willing the burn.

The fire on her hands and coursing through her scars got hotter and hotter until she felt like she couldn't take it anymore. She opened her eyes and looked at her hands. Brilliant white and gold light shimmered, making it hard to see. She slowly pulled them apart, and a rainbow of color shot straight up. It was beautiful and awe-inspiring. She looked from the rainbow brilliance back to the gold outline and started to trace the golden portal outline, willing it away. The screaming and hoarse cries of pain erupted from all around her. She ignored them and concentrated on standing upright despite the clenching in her stomach that was intensifying. Holding fast, she traced along the edges of the portal's gold perimeter. It was nearly two thirds of the way closed, yet she felt her strength diminishing. Suddenly she felt another fiery heat source next to her. She glanced over and saw her mom, standing next to her, with a golden white glow and equally brilliant rainbow pouring upwards from her hand. Her mom was helping her close the portal!

With renewed vigor, Gabriella concentrated even harder and kept tracing. She was shaking and her vision was blurring. She didn't think she could stand much more. The effort was taking a toll and she wanted to let her entire body drop to the ground. Her mom by her side was the only thing that kept her going.

She traced over the last remaining gold section and met her mom's intersecting light. She stood there for a few seconds longer, enduring the brilliance and heat, then dropped her hands. They cooled to normal temperature almost immediately, and the light and rainbow disappeared. It was over. The portal was closed.

Gabriella dropped to her knees and put her elbows, hands and head on the ground. She was exhausted and ravenously hungry all at the same time. Then she felt her mom's arms encircle her and pull her halfway into her lap and hug her.

"You did it, Gabriella. You closed the portal. I only helped you finish it," her mom's soft, warm voice whispered into her ear. Tears leaked out of Gabby's closed eyes and streamed down her cheeks. She'd missed her mom so much, and she wanted to soak in the feel of her warmth and the smell of her. She ignored everything else and just breathed in her mom's scent. In this moment, she knew for certain. She was her mother's daughter, an alchemist just like her mom.

After a few moments, her mom lifted her chin. "Gabriella, open your eyes."

Gabby opened them up and looked at her mom. Hunter came up from behind and handed a piece of cheese to her mother. With a nod of thanks, her mom took the cheese and handed it to Gabby. "Eat this, then stand up," her mom told her.

Gabriella ate the cheese and looked beyond her mom. The Dark army was surrounding them, but Hunter, Wyatt and Cayden were standing right next to them. The horses were lying on the ground, lifeless and bloody, similar to their horses earlier in the morning. Gabriella sucked in her breath at the sight and pushed up from her mom's lap, standing up.

"The horses, what happened to the horses?" she asked.

Her mom shook her head. "You drew from them, Gabriella. You had no metal to use, so you drew from them any metal they had inside their bodies," her mom explained sadly as she pulled Gabriella to her feet.

Once Gabriella stood, she looked around and realized just how many horses had suffered a bloody fate. Feeling flushed and nauseous, she swayed and her vision blurred as tears started to form in her eyes. The desire to cry out was strong, yet she held it inside.

The army parted to let someone or something through. The Dark King marched toward them, with the Light King next to him. Both had stern, closed expressions on their faces. Beside the Light King strode Uncle Robert. He smiled briefly at Gabby before turning his attention back to the situation at hand.

# CHAPTER TWENTY-FOUR

"You did this, girl?" The Dark King glowered at Gabby.

Gabriella stared up at him. Her mom stood next to her and put a hand on her shoulder. Before she could respond or stand, Holden appeared in front of her.

"Leave my sister alone," he growled at the Dark King, pointing his dagger up at him.

The Dark King gave a bark of laughter.

"Do you think to threaten me, boy?" He glanced down at Holden.

Holden opened his mouth to answer but before he could speak, the small dragon jumped from behind him and roared at the Dark King. Around them, leprechauns pointed their swords at the dragon. It roared again, standing on its back two legs, ready to fight.

"No, down!" Holden told the dragon, but kept his dagger pointed at the Dark King. The dragon fell back to all fours, but kept a sharpened set of eyes trained on the king.

"Interesting," the Dark King said, but made no other move or statement.

A movement sent ripples through the mass of people standing at the front of the battle. The appearance of the two goblins, Gildseth and Bentley, caused the crowd of soldiers to turn their attention toward them. They walked up and stood next to the Light King. Bentley leaned forward and whispered something in the king's ear. The Light King listened and then nodded. Bentley turned to address the crowd gathered before him.

"We, the goblins, vouch for the lineage of the children that stand before you all. The children are of both the Light and Dark royal houses." At his announcement, a sea of startled gasps rushed through all three armies.

"My grandchildren?" the Dark King said, looking down at Holden, then at Gabriella.

"I'm not your grandchild." Gabriella scowled at him. This battle was his fault; he was the one who had imprisoned her mom. She wanted nothing to do with this man.

"You are, Gabriella." Her mom stepped forward, rubbing her wrists. The ropes had left raw, angry burn marks.

"What? How can I be? He's awful. He wanted to invade the human realm! I'm not his granddaughter! I refuse to be!" Gabriella was angry and exhausted. She and the boys had tossed about the idea that her father was a royal leprechaun, Prince of the Dark Leprechauns, but this made it true. What made it worse was that her mom had kept this secret from her. "Then how do I have these scars, if I'm a leprechaun and not human at all? I shouldn't have these scars!"

Her mom's eyes widened, but she didn't have a chance to respond, as the Light King stepped forward.

"Gabriella," her other grandfather, the Light King, spoke her name in warning. She looked at him, then at her mom.

"Why? How?" she asked.

"Yes, why? And where is my son?" the Dark King demanded as he stepped toward her mother. Holden lifted his dagger higher and kept it pointed at him.

"Do you really think to threaten me with that, boy?" the Dark King repeated, lifting his eyebrows at Holden.

"No, grandfather" Holden smirked up at the man. "If you mean to threaten my mom, I mean to use it." Holden glared up at the Dark King. His angry expression dared the Dark King to engage him. Gabriella had never seen her brother acting so militant.

The Dark King regarded him for a moment, with an obscure look. He nodded, yet didn't step back. "I'm not threatening your mom. I want answers. As I am sure you do also."

"Not right now, I don't," Holden answered. "Gabriella, are you okay?" he asked, his gaze never leaving his grandfather.

"Yes, yes, I'm fine." Gabriella turned her hands over, looking at them. They looked normal, and they didn't feel hot like they had before she closed the portal. In slow motion, she reached up and touched the side of her face. Her scars were not hot anymore either, feeling like they always had.

"It appears we have common ground," the Light King addressed the Dark King, "more common than ever before and more important."

"Agreed," the Dark King said.

Someone else stepped forward and removed the helm he was wearing. "I propose that we stand down the armies and have a council meeting, to sort out a few outstanding issues." The man who spoke was dressed in gray and blue, from his helm down to his leather boots. A creature rising out of the sea was on the crest on the front of his chest.

Gabriella looked up at what she assumed was the Ash King. He had sandy blond hair and was much younger than the other two High Kings. He wore lighter shades than the other kings. His army was awash in the same blue and gray colors.

"Agreed," the Dark King uttered again and nodded.

"A council meeting it is. Shall we say, in a half hour's time?" the Light King proposed.

"My receiving chambers will be readied," the Dark King said, with a short nod. He looked down at Holden. "Will you accompany me, boy, to assist with preparations for the meeting?"

Holden almost dropped his dagger. Gabriella looked at Holden. She could see that he'd been ready to stab this man just moments before, fear and anger coursing through him, and now he was being asked to join him in a menial task. She watched as he looked back at their mom, then at their Uncle Robert, standing next to the Light King.

"Go. Assist your grandfather. We'll talk later about this dragon of yours," Uncle Robert told him, gesturing to the little dragon standing guard next to Holden.

Gabriella watched her brother as he tried to keep his emotions from showing on his face. She understood what he was feeling. Only two days before, they'd never met any other family but their uncle and now they had two Grandfathers, cousins and others. It was an odd feeling, and one she wasn't sure he liked yet. She sighed as Holden took a step back from their grandfather and sheathed his dagger.

His dragon hissed up at the Dark King. The Dark King ignored it, but she could see his cheek muscles clench.

"Only if Wyatt and Hunter may help too," Holden demanded. If his request surprised the Dark King, it didn't show. The king nodded.

"And my dragon comes with me." Holden put his hand on the dragon's head.

The Dark King ignored this last statement and walked toward the Dark Castle. Holden gave a quick glance toward Gabriella and his mom, then turned and followed his grandfather. Wyatt and Hunter fell into step on either side of him. They both had surprised expressions on their faces, yet both also wore small smiles.

Gabriella looked up at her mom. "I closed the portal. I really did it."

"I'm so very proud of you, Gabriella." Her mom wrapped her arms around her and hugged tightly. "Believe me, I never wanted any of this to happen or for you to find out the way you did. I've been trying to protect you, maybe trying a little too hard."

"I know, mom. I have so many questions, but for right now, I'm just glad you're okay." Gabriella hugged her mom back, trying not cry. She missed the way her mom smelled, missed the way she talked, missed her hugs, missed everything about her. She was so happy to have her back.

"We have a lot to talk about, Gabriella, and it is going to be difficult for a while. You and your brother just showed three kingdoms the immense power you possess. You are not yet of age, and have abilities far beyond most of our kind. That is going to create a bit of fear that will need to be addressed. You will also need to be trained and learn more about the leprechaun ways." Her mom stepped back, yet kept her hands on Gabby's shoulders.

"Why can't we just go home, back to Minnesota?" Gabriella asked.

"Because, Gabriella, that has never really been home. This is home," her mom told her. Her eyes were sad. "I was running away and trying to protect you. I also thought that if I raised you with humans, you would have empathy for them. Which you do. You proved that today by closing the portal and stopping your grandfather's army from invading."

"He was only invading to come after my dad," Gabriella said, not sure why she was defending a man she didn't know. He didn't really feel like her dad. Plus, he wasn't alive so it didn't really matter.

"Yet he was still intent on invading," her mom said.

"How're you doing, Sprite?" Uncle Robert walked over and ruffled her hair, like he had done so many times when she was younger. Normally she'd huff at him and complain that he was messing up her hair. Right now though, the action felt good, comfortable, something she knew.

"I'm doing okay. Just a lot to take in," she told him. She still didn't understand. She was the daughter of a Light Princess and Dark Prince. She'd thought it was bad enough when she was half human and half leprechaun. That she was full leprechaun still didn't make sense.

"I understand that. I've always suspected you weren't quite what you seemed." Her uncle smiled down at her. "You met Tay?" he asked, his eyes lighting up at the mention of his daughter.

"Yes!" Gabriella said, loud enough for the breaking armies to notice. "She's awesome. I have a cousin. Why didn't you ever tell me?" she demanded.

"Your mother and I needed to come to an understanding, which we had not done yet. I wanted to tell you, but never found the right moment," he said, although his smile turned down a bit. He shook his head at his sister. "Jeremias, really?"

Her mom shot her uncle a glare. "Later, Robert."

"Oh, you bet, later. Father is going to have some words for you." Her jokester uncle's eyes gleamed at her mom. Her mom continued to glare back at him.

Gabriella folded her arms across her chest. "And you get mad at Holden and me for arguing with each other?"

Her mom stopped glaring at her uncle and started laughing. "Yeah, you two shouldn't fight. You're brother and sister."

Her uncle wagged his eyebrows at his sister. "See?" he said, continuing the exaggerated eyebrow wagging.

Her mom rolled her eyes at him. "Don't you have an army to attend to?"

Her uncle's expression became serious. "I do. We will chat later, once the army has moved toward the mountain a bit and settled to make camp for the night. We'll also talk more after the council meeting." He gave his sister a hug, gave Gabriella one also, then turned and headed back to his army.

The Ash King and her grandfather, the Light King, were standing together talking. Gabriella looked up at her mom. "The Ash King, is he good or bad?"

Gabriella's mom looked down at her. "Gabby, no one is only good or only bad. Everyone has qualities that are both good and bad. It is the decisions you make, how you treat people and what you do when both no one and everyone is looking."

"Great, Mom, now you sound like a ridiculous quote of the day." She rolled her eyes.

Her mom put an arm around her shoulders and steered her in the direction of both High Kings. "Now the Ash King, even though he has only been ruling for about five hundred years, he's been a good King to his people and helps, along with your grandfather, the Light King, to keep the treaty with other realms."

"Your majesties," her mother addressed both kings and gave a quick, short bow. Gabriella kept silent but mimicked her by dipping into a short bow also.

"Shay. Gabriella." The Light King nodded at them both. The Ash King did likewise.

"I think you both should attend the council meeting this time," the Ash King said. "There will be items discussed that will pertain to you, along with questions that need to be asked. It is better to ask one question and get one answer than for many to ask the same questions repeatedly."

Her mom sighed. "I know. I understand I have a lot to explain."

"Not to apologize for, just to explain," the Light King interjected. Then he pulled his daughter into a tight hug. "I've missed you so very much, Shay."

"I've missed you too, Father," her mom said, muffled against her father's leather armor.

They hugged tightly for a few more moments before her grandfather looked down at her mom. "Decisions will be made, Shay. We will get through them, but decisions must be made."

"I understand. I know I've been running from these decisions for far too long," her mom said.

Trumpets sounded from the Dark Castle. The huge metal portcullis that had been closed began to rise. It was the signal that the council meeting of the High Kings was about to begin.

# CHAPTER TWENTY-FIVE

Gabriella followed her mother, grandfather, and the Ash King through the raised portcullis and into the outer bailey of the Dark Castle. She looked down and realized she was wearing the cloak of the Dark and dress of the Light. She had donned the green colors two days earlier, as more of a costume. The black cloak she acquired only yesterday for warmth, yet now they had become a part of her outfit. She saw the irony of her clothes. They represented a mixing of houses between her mother and newly discovered grandfather.

As their party wound their way through the bailey and into the castle, Cayden fell into step with Gabriella. She hadn't seen him since their race to the portal, as the Dark army had been preparing to invade and the other armies had been battling.

"Hello, official cousin." Cayden smiled at her. He handed her an apple. She felt like she could eat ten apples at the moment.

Her mom looked back at them and saw Gabriella eating the apple. "Oh, Gabby, I'm sorry," she told her. "Portal magic draws a lot from you, and you're going to need a lot to eat over the next few hours. Thank you," she said to Cayden. He nodded at her and kept walking with them.

"Strange that we are related, isn't it?" Gabriella asked between mouthfuls of apple.

"Not really, "Cayden told her. "What is strange is that it never really felt like you and Holden were strangers."

"Yeah, that is true. You guys never felt like strangers either," Gabriella agreed.

They came to a large room, with guards on either side of the door. The guards opened the doors and ushered them through. Gabriella looked up as they stepped inside. The room was about three stories high, with armor and crimson tapestries hanging on the walls. A large table stood in the middle and looked like it could seat at least seventy grown men. Holden and her other grandfather were standing at the end. Wyatt and Hunter, and their two other brothers, Ian and Jhett, were standing a bit off to the side of them, on their right.

The Dark King motioned for them to sit down at the end of the table, near him. As the Dark King sat at the head of the table, the Ash King took the place to his right while the Light King took the seat to his left. Gabriella waited until her mom sat next to the Light King, then sat next to her mom. Holden walked over and settled next to Gabriella.

"How'd it go?" Gabby leaned over and whispered to him.

"Fine. It was a little odd. Wyatt, Hunter and I didn't really do anything. We stood around until Ian and Jhett showed up. They spoke with Grandfather for a few moments. Then Grandfather had food brought in and we sat down to eat." Holden gestured to the large platters of food in the center of the table. There were different types of bread, assorted cheeses, berries, grapes, and roasted meats.

The Dark King motioned to his nephews. Cayden, Hunter, Wyatt, Jhett and Ian all stood, nodded and left the room. Holden stood to follow them.

"Holden, you and Gabriella will remain for this council meeting," the Dark King said. Holden sat back down. The Dark King looked at Gabby and gestured to the food. Gabriella didn't hesitate; she reached over and took some meat, cheese and grapes, shoving them in her mouth as fast as she could chew. Holden also selected some bread and cheese.

"I have one main question." The Dark King looked directly at Gabby's mom. "Where's my son?"

Gabriella's mom looked at the Dark King. "Banished. To the land of dragons," she said, not mincing words.

The Dark King stood. "Banished to the land of dragons!" he bellowed. His face turned a mottled red and he slammed his fist down on the wooden table. "How was he banished to the land of dragons?"

Gabby's mom jumped to her feet. She pointed at her chest. "I sent him there, to protect my children," she told the Dark King, giving him a hard glare.

"Daughter," the Light King said, "Alaric. Please sit back down and let's discuss how Jeremias came to be banished to the land of dragons."

After a few tense moments, Gabriella's mom sat back down and the Dark King did also, although the Dark King was not as graceful. He fell into his chair with a clatter.

"Shay, please explain why you would banish the Dark Prince," the Ash King ordered.

"When I found out I was pregnant with Gabriella, Jeremias and I decided that we didn't want to hide anymore, living together only for brief amounts of time in the borderlands. We'd been secretly married for many months, and knew that we could not live in either the Dark Kingdom or the Light Kingdom. We both agreed that it would be a good idea to live in the human world, until we could approach both kingdoms and find a balance. I would have been happy living in the borderlands, but Jeremias was not. For the first year, living in the human world was wonderful. But then Jeremias became frustrated with people. He looked down on them, believed he was better than they were and increasingly became bitter. He wanted to return to the Dark Kingdom and bring Gabriella with him. We had many heated disagreements over this. Jeremias became cruel in his dealings with humans. He said he agreed with his father and that he was going to return with his daughter. When she was of age, he intended to break the treaty of humans.

"On the day of our last argument, a horrible one, he demanded that I open a portal to the Dark Kingdom. He was furious. He grabbed Gabriella and wouldn't let her go. He threatened to hurt her unless I opened a portal. I refused, not believing he would hurt his own child. But he lifted her high, then dropped her. She fell to the ground and began shrieking. Again he demanded that I open a portal or he would hurt her worse. So I did. Except it wasn't a portal to the Dark Kingdom; it was a portal to the land of dragons. I'd already picked up Gabriella and was backing away. Jeremias started to step through the portal when he sensed that something was wrong, that it wasn't to the Dark Kingdom. He grabbed for Gabriella as he went through. Gabriella fell against the molten gold of the portal opening's arch, and that's how she was burned and scarred." Gabriella touched the side of her face, feeling the scars. She wondered if that's why they heated up also, when her hands became hot. Because the scars were caused by portal gold. Not by a burning house fire, as she'd previously believed.

Her mother continued, "I pulled her back with me. Jeremias fell through the portal. Then I closed it. Gabriella was still shrieking and crying. It took a long time to calm her down and I feared for her life, the burn was so bad. I was pregnant with Holden at the time, but neither I nor Jeremias knew it then. The children believed their father died in a fire. Gabriella remembered fire and I never dissuaded her." Shay looked down, as if contrite.

"To hurt a child, in particular a leprechaun child, is a grave offense," the Ash King said.

"And my son? Is he still in the land of the dragons?" The Dark King ignored the Ash King's statement and directed his question at their mother. He stood up and turned his back to the table.

"He might be. I never opened a portal back," Shay confirmed.

The Dark King lifted his head and roared, "No one can survive on their own there, not even a leprechaun! The dragons would rip him apart."

Shay lowered her head. "I know," she whispered. "For that reason, I remained in the human world, and exiled myself and the children from the leprechaun realm. Even though Gabriella was wounded, his loss still was a loss."

"You destroyed my son!" the Dark King barked, keeping his back to the table.

"I protected my child!"

"My grandchildren remain with me, they are all that remains of my son," the Dark King said, his back still turned to the table. His voice was lower.

Holden and Gabriella stopped eating, then looked at their mother. She wore a stunned expression. "Never!" she retorted. "You will never get my children!"

"Enough," the Light King said. "As children of both royal houses, they are extremely important to both kingdoms. Their upbringing should have happened in the leprechaun realm, yet it did not. This needs to be rectified. The children should spend time in each kingdom, with the ways and customs of our peoples, and learning to control and refine their abilities. One day, they will be leaders and they need to be prepared to handle that mantle."

The Dark King half turned and nodded in silent agreement. He finished turning fully around and both he and the Light King looked to the Ash King.

"I propose more of an equal balance," the Ash King said. "I will also foster them. They should spend time with all the royal houses until they are of age. Then they will make the decision as to which royal house, the Dark or the Light, they want to reside in."

"This does not mean I agree with the human treaty, nor absolve your daughter of the destruction of my son," the Dark King told the Light King. "Yet I agree the children are extremely powerful and should not belong solely to one royal house. I am in agreement with these terms."

"The Light Princess defended her child. Her actions were justified, even if you don't agree with them. The Dark Prince struck, in anger, at a child, for his own means," the Ash King said to the Dark King.

"Alleged actions," the Dark King argued.

"You have the word of a royal. That is sufficient," the Light King reminded him. "You also opened an invading portal to the human realm. Had your army entered, war would have been imminent."

"We resolve these matters now," the Ash King counseled the other two kings. "There was no loss of life today, the human realm remains untouched, and the children have been recovered. I propose we close this council, and resolve to meet, as three once again, at the next scheduled council."

The Light and Dark Kings glowered at each other. They both nodded in silence.

"The Light Princess had the children until this point. Their stay starts at the Dark realm," the Dark King said forcefully. "Plus, we also have to address the issue of a boy and a dragon," he nodded toward the dragon curled up, sleeping next to where Holden sat.

"Why not a few hours here today, then let them stay with their mother for a period of time. They did come a long way to find her, and risked much," the Ash King said, looking carefully toward the Dark King.

Hearing no disagreement, the Ash King continued, "We've kept to our own kingdoms for too long. This proves it. We should attempt to move between kingdoms more, and these children give cause as to why. My own children would do well to get to know all kingdoms better. Why not allow the children a few weeks in each, rather than long stays that keep them away too long from any particular one?"

The Dark King stood still. "One of them will be my heir," he said in a lowered voice.

"One of them will be my heir also," the Light King matched his tone.

"All the more reason to finish raising them between kingdoms," the Ash King said. Gabriella looked between her grandfathers. She'd never considered that she'd live anywhere other than back in the human world and suddenly, she was going to be living in different kingdoms, and quite soon. It made her head spin.

The Light King took a deep breath, nodded and said, "As we all agree, this council meeting is at a close."

All three kings nodded at each other. Gabriella looked at her brother, who sat in silence. He stared back at her, both of them unsure of what to do next. They were staying in the Dark Kingdom, with a grandfather they did not know. No one had asked their opinion. She wished they would have.

Their mother stood, leaned over and gave Gabby a crushing hug." I love you," she told her. "I'm going to step outside, with my father."

"Mom, does that mean we're staying here?" Gabriella asked.

Her mom only nodded, and walked over to Holden and gave him an equally crushing hug.

"I love you two and will see you in a bit." Gabriella watched her give her brother a kiss on the head before she released him. She ruffled his hair, then turned and accompanied her father and the Ash King out of the chamber.

Gabriella and Holden watched her go. There will still so many unanswered questions, such as why she came to the Dark Kingdom in the first place and how she'd been captured. The questions would have to wait, because their stay in the Dark Kingdom had just begun. If only for a few hours. They were leprechauns now, and not humans.

The dragon nudged between the two of them. Gabriella slowly trailed her hand along the scales on its back.

Their new grandfather turned to them. He pointed down at the dragon.

"A dragon? In my kingdom?" he asked.

Holden grinned. He reached over and patted the dragon on the head. The dragon lifted its head and he moved his hand down and scratched it under the chin.

"It's our pet dragon," Gabriella said, still wary of the man.

"Yes, it appears so." Her grandfather looked at her.

She crossed her arms over her chest and lifted her chin, defiant. Her grandfather mimicked her actions. He crossed his arms over his chest and stared down at her. She held his gaze.

"Well," her grandfather said as a slow smile spread across his face, "have you a name for your dragon?"

Gabriella let her hands drop and smiled back at him. She looked at Holden. He smiled at her. Their grandfather might not be so bad after all. She looked back up at him.

"DKD," she said, and her eyes crinkled with delight.

"That's an interesting name," her grandfather said.

"Yeah, it means Dark King's Dragon," Gabriella said and Holden burst out laughing next to her. Their grandfather joined them.

Maybe her mom was right. People weren't always good or bad. She and her brother had entered the leprechaun realm to find their mom. They'd done all they could to get to her. That didn't make them bad, even though some of their actions might not be considered good. Her grandfather was trying to find his son, her father. He was doing what was within his power. His actions might not have been good, yet that didn't make him bad. They all were trying to do what they thought best.

She was curious to get to know her grandfather.

# CHAPTER TWENTY-SIX

He reached up and pushed his hand through the portal. It hadn't closed yet. It would soon, as happened to all unauthorized portals. He slid his hand around the gold perimeter, testing the size. Because his daughter had been halted in the middle of the creation, it wasn't very big, but it was still open. It didn't have to be very large, just enough for him to fit through.

Satisfied, he stepped back down from the large rock he'd been standing on and something large slammed against his side. He turned around and pushed the small black dragon away. The dragon hissed in response but moved back, lumbering and twisting as it did. Its ebony gaze followed. There was only the one dragon. His twin brother wasn't with him. The two dragons spent their waking and sleeping moments together and were rarely apart.

After their mother had died from wounds sustained in a fight, he'd raised them from hatchlings. She'd been his constant companion for the majority of the years he'd been in the dragon wasteland. Her death had been a loss that he still felt. When you spent years with another creature, nearly every waking moment, it was hard recovering from that loss. His aching grief had been lessened by the egg she'd left behind. The surprise at not just one dragon hatchling, but two from the same egg had turned to joy. He'd been the first thing they saw, touched and felt, and they had quickly bonded to him. As they grew, he'd created images of their mother, to teach them to fly, to hunt, to fight.

In his youth, dragons were creatures that were captured and forced back to the dragon realm. They were seen as wild, uncontrollable beings and no leprechaun had ever tried to tame or befriend one. His banishment had forced him to see dragons with a different view. Living amongst them changed his mind. Their mother had been a young dragon when he'd come across her, mere days after his arrival in the dragon realm. Her chest had been gouged by another dragon and she was dying. Instead of finishing the work of the other dragon, he'd nursed her back to health. In the following years, she'd grown massive and become an alpha dragon.

The small dragon nudged him with its snout, ending his memories. He stroked the dragon's head.

"You can't come this trip, but soon enough," he told the dragon, his voice soothing and low. "Soon enough."

He pushed the dragon back and stood, stretching both arms above him and grasping both sides of the portal. Straining, he pulled himself up and through the opening. He kicked his legs and propelled his body forward until he was in the next realm.

He felt the cool, dewy crisp grass and pressed his face in the lush fragrance. The land he'd been in for the past thirteen years was dry, dusty and arid. The dragons burned most of the vegetation and the craggy, steep hills they perched in were gleaming obsidian monstrosities.

Compared to that terrain, the feel and smell of the grass was incredible and he lay there for a moment. It tickled his cheeks and he began to chuckle. His deep voice rolled through the meadow. He laughed harder and turned on his back, to look up at the bright, blue skies above him. A few thick, puffy clouds dotted the view.

He didn't want to move and ruin his homecoming. He wanted to stretch out the serene moment. A soft wisp of a seed twisting through the light breeze blew across his line of vision. He stood up, dusted off his crudely made leather trousers and held himself back from running to the road that led up the mountain. For many years, he thought he'd never see the mountain of home or vibrant green trees again. There would be a lot of time for sightseeing once he arrived at the castle. He'd learned patience and perseverance. A long walk, in the lush land of his birth would be a soothing prelude to his homecoming.

A small roar sounded above him. He looked up and the younger of the twin dragons was circling above.

He laughed. "Well, I guess soon wasn't quick enough for you," he called up to the scaly beast that had followed him through the portal. The opening would need to be closed, to prevent additional dragons from entering, but he wasn't too worried. Only the smaller, younger dragons could fit through and those were of no concern to him.

He motioned down with his two forefingers and the little dragon flew to land next him with a light thud. "Where's your brother, little buddy?" he asked.

The dragon only blinked. He hadn't really expected a response. Over the past decade, he'd gotten used to one-sided conversations.

He snapped his fingers and the dragon followed, slithering along next to him. He quickened his pace. It was time to go home. He'd been away much too long.

Jeremias was back.

# ACKNOWLEDGEMENTS

Amie, sisters like you are rare. Very few would move thousands of miles away to help raise children, to be a partner in adventures and malarkey, and stand by your side at the most difficult of times. Above all, you've always believed in me and while you may not have always agreed, you encouraged me to be myself and to pursue my own path. Since childhood, you've been the ear for my imagination. Heidi, sometimes out of darkness come bright, beautiful things. That's our friendship and that is you. Jerry, for writing with me, listening to me talk about plots and ideas, and being part of this fantasy world in the wee hours of the morning. Carlos, first a colleague, then mentor and friend. You give me incredible advice and this story would have never moved forward had you not encouraged me when I needed it most. Kim, thank you for being my biggest leprechaun anti-cheerleader cheerleader.

To the real life Gabriella and Holden, always remember this world is filled with magic and never stop seeking the good in others, and in yourself.

And Ian – you believed in me. You pushed me out of my comfort zone and past my safety net. You made this happen.

# ABOUT THE AUTHOR

Carolyn Killion — A bit of a dreamer but a do'er. Head is in the clouds, but feet firmly on the ground. A list maker, cookie baker, perpetual student of string theory, bumbling hiker, cavorting canoeist, fantastical writer, erstwhile fisher, winter sun midday napper, thirsty seeker of knowledge, eager traveler. Lives in Grantsburg, WI.